A Medical Thriller by

VICTOR METHOS

Men die of the diseases which they have studied most.

— Sir Arthur Conan Doyle

1

Four o'clock in the morning, the man sprinted down the terminal, his heart pounding like a drum.

He glanced back once and saw the walls of O'Hare International pressing in around him. A bathroom was to the right, and he ran inside and went straight to a stall. He closed and locked the door and then climbed onto the toilet so his feet weren't visible underneath the door. Sweat was pouring out of him so profusely that he could barely see out of his glasses, and he took them off and wiped them on his shirt.

His vision was still blurry, and he wiped his glasses again before he realized tears were obscuring his view. He thought of his wife and wondered what she was doing right then. He hadn't had time to get her. And even if he could have, he knew she wouldn't be safe. But leaving her back in Los Angeles might've been signing her death warrant, too. He didn't know what the right decision was.

A couple of people were in the bathroom, and the sounds of their voices calmed him. But then he heard a set of purposeful and calm footfalls walk in, sending a shiver up his spine. He held his breath.

The footsteps grew closer, and he quietly slipped off the toilet and looked under the stall. A pair of black crocodile-skin dress shoes stood at the first stall. The door opened, then they moved on to the second stall.

The man got down on his belly. He was in the fifth stall. He crawled into the sixth and then the seventh. Someone opened the eighth and stepped inside. He couldn't risk a confrontation. He looked back and crawled the other way.

The shoes got to the fifth stall, and their owner tried the door, which was locked. The crocodile-skin wing-tips stood quietly a moment before standing up on tiptoe.

As the shoes moved on to the next one, the man crawled over into the fifth stall. He had timed it well enough, he thought. He kept going. All the other stalls were empty up to the first, and he crawled until he got there and then got to his feet and peeked out. No one was around him, so he slipped out and headed outside, when a hand rested on his shoulder.

He spun around and batted the hand away, but a blow to his chest sucked all the wind out of him. Another blow flung him back against the sinks. He hit his head on the mirror, shattering it.

"No, please," he begged. He thought of his wife, and the tears flowed.

The attacker held him by his collar as he cried. He was handsome and young, and he wore a black suit—not at all how the man had thought his killer would look.

"Do you want money?" the man said, sensing the killer's hesitation. "I have plenty of it. Enough for you to retire on today. I can get it for you right now." His glasses had flown off, and he could see only a hazy outline. "Whatever they paid you to kill me, I'll pay you ten times more. Twenty times."

"Do you know," the man said in a calm, steely voice, "how many people you've put at risk?"

"What was I supposed to do?" he said, beginning to cry again. "Just lie down and die? Even a dog wouldn't do that."

"I wouldn't actually care, except for one thing. You are a hindrance to my employer's plans."

The killer took out a pistol with a silencer attached.

"Wait! Wait. Please wait. You're... you're Ian, right? That's what they call you. Ian. I know about you. I knew you were the one they would send after me. Ian, please, I have a wife. I have a wife, and that's why I did this. I can't watch her die."

"You won't."

He pulled the trigger, and the man's brains and bits of skull spattered against the broken mirror. Blood spread out in a lotus pattern behind him, and a red halo appeared to be hovering above him.

A toilet flushed, and Ian turned around to see an older black man standing at the stall.

"I didn't see nothin'," he said.

"That's right. You didn't."

Ian shot him twice in the chest as he walked out of the bathroom. He took out his iPhone once he was in the terminal and opened a dossier. Inside was a list of names and locations, along with birthdays and current photos. He ran his finger across the name at the top: Norman Russell Stewart. His name and information turned to a light gray, then faded into the background. Six names were left on the list.

Ian tucked the phone into his pocket, then left the terminal.

2

Dr. Samantha Bower stood on top of the Hotel Intercontinental in Kinshasa, the tallest building in the Democratic Republic of the Congo. The wind was strong that day, and she felt its warmth against her sunburnt face as she looked out over the city.

The city was surprisingly modern, despite the poverty and horror that surrounded it. Office buildings and billboards gave it a sense that it was attempting to catch up with the rest of the modern world, but its gray, menacing fog permeated everyone. Not sixty miles from where she stood, nearly an entire village had been slaughtered by the FDLR, a rebel military force. They had raped the women, some as old as eighty and as young as two, in front of the men. Then they mutilated them so they could never reproduce. Many times, the husbands and fathers of the women were held at gunpoint, forced to partake in the rape and torture.

Nothing more than terrorism on a grand scale, it had been dubbed "the Forgotten Conflict" by United Nations workers. Over five million people had died, and no one seemed to even know what was really going on.

As horrific as the FDLR was, she was there for another killer. Her killer was more prolific, more deceitful, and far more deadly.

An outbreak of Ebola hemorrhagic fever had been reported less than three days before at the Kinshasa General Hospital. Though it was the country's busiest and best-equipped hospital, its staff hadn't taken proper precautions for containment. The staff simply hadn't known what they had, even though an outbreak of Ebola in 1976 had killed nearly three hundred people.

Samantha pulled out her phone using her good hand—one of her wrists had been broken the month before and was still in a cast—and checked her e-mail. She found twelve unread e-mails from the Centers for Disease Control and two from an epidemiologist in Bakwanga, the Congo's second-largest city, as well as a text from her boyfriend, Duncan, that said, *Be careful.*

She stepped down from her perch and turned back toward the entrance to the hospital. Though Ebola was destructive, she knew of something even deadlier. And her initial concern, before testing proved otherwise, was that this outbreak was deadlier than Ebola.

Black pox—more specifically, a new strain that the CDC had termed Agent X—spread in a way she had never seen. As far as she knew, it was the world's number-one killer, and some speculation, which had vaguely begun in an unfinished article by her former boss Dr. Ralph Wilson before his death, had made the rounds that the Plague of Justinian, the deadliest epidemic in history, may have been black pox rather than bubonic plague.

And just one month earlier, an outbreak of black pox had held the world by the throat. After the nightmare of the first outbreak was over, Samantha debated whether or not she wished to continue working at the CDC. In the end, it was a matter of expedience. She wanted to work with hot viruses—ones that were extremely deadly and contagious—and nowhere, with the exception of the military, would she have more freedom to do so. But working with the CDC came with a downside: she knew things in advance that the general public was not allowed to know.

Walking inside the hospital, she went down to the sixth floor, a wing normally reserved for psychiatric patients. In almost any hospital, the psychiatric ward was the easiest to clear. She walked to the empty nurse's station and sat in a chair, then stretched her legs. She calmed herself with breathing exercises. After being attacked and brutally beaten in her home—the cast was the last spectacle from the incident—public places gave her a gnawing anxiety that forced her to consciously control her reactions. She also carried a small stone with her that she rubbed whenever the anxiety came on.

Wearing full biohazard gear, a tall doctor named We Kayembe came out of one of the hospital rooms. He went into the temporary shower that had been set up in the bathroom, and Samantha heard the water bouncing off the biohazard suit.

Dr. Kayembe came out in sweatpants a short while later and sat down about fifteen feet from her, behind the transparent plastic barrier that had been installed the night before.

He had been infected with Ebola and was beginning to look worse. Nineteen patients, all with confirmed Ebola, were in this wing of the hospital, and Dr. Kayembe continued to treat them. Samantha knew he wore the suit just to avoid cross-contamination in case they were carrying anything other than Ebola. She appreciated the fact that he was concerned with such things, considering that when she'd arrived, the Ebola patients had filled beds in the emergency room, without barriers around them.

"You look tired," he said in his deep voice that was accented heavily with French. "Have you slept?"

"Not for thirty-six hours. You?"

"No. I can't sleep. I have nightmares."

She was silent a moment. "Do you need anything?"

"A new body?" he joked.

She smiled out of obligation, but humor was the last thing she felt.

In the past thirty-six hours, she had seen a woman vomit so much black blood that her skin had turned a pasty white before death and she didn't have enough left in her body to fill a syringe. She had seen a young boy of no more than twelve tear open the skin on his legs and torso by doing nothing more than sitting up in bed. His skin had liquefied and slipped off his body, and he'd bled to death. And she had seen a pregnant woman lose her baby one day and her life the next.

And Dr. Kayembe, who was newly infected, displayed pharyngitis, a severe inflammation of the throat, as well as an irritation of his eyes' mucous membranes, abdominal cramping, and vomiting, though he had not yet begun to vomit blood.

"You know, I learned English in school," he said. "I never got to see the United States, though."

"Your English is very good. Better than mine, actually."

He smiled. "I love English, but French I love more. Even when you swear and talk about wiping your ass, it is like poetry... Do you have any children?"

"No."

"Have children. Plenty of them. That is my most profound regret. That I did not have any. No one will remember me after this."

She was quiet. "I'll remember you."

He smiled weakly and rubbed the bridge of his nose. "I'm going to go lie down."

"It's not a hundred percent fatal," she blurted out as he rose, regretting doing so as soon as the words came out, but it was too late. He was looking at her. "Ebola's mortality rate is around seventy percent. It's not a guaranteed death sentence."

He nodded and then went into a room at the end of the hall.

Samantha exhaled and leaned her head against the wall. The outbreak had been contained after leaving forty-two people dead and nineteen more that would probably die in the next week or so. She was there to fill out paperwork and submit her findings to the CDC, which would then submit them to the World Health Organization.

Her cell phone buzzed and her boyfriend's name appeared on the screen.

"Hey," she answered.

"Hey," he replied after a slight delay from the distance. "How's everything there?"

"As awful as you'd think. I don't want to talk about here, though. Tell me what's happening there. What happened on *Game of Thrones* yesterday?"

"A lot of nudity and violence."

"I'll take that over what I'm seeing any day."

A pause. "I shouldn't tell you this. We're... well..."

"What is it?"

As a researcher with the United States Army Medical Research Institute for Infectious Diseases, Duncan, from time to time, had information that no one, not even the CDC, had access to.

"Your sister's in California right now, right?"

"Yeah, Disneyland."

"How long is she going to be there?"

"I'm not sure, couple more days, I guess. Why?"

Duncan paused. "Get her out now."

"What d'you mean 'get her out'?"

"I mean call her right now, right after you hang up with me, and tell her that she has to be on the next plane out. If she waits until morning, it's too late."

"Why? What's going on, Duncan?"

"Not on the phone. When are you going to be home?"

"I have a flight in a few hours."

"Come see me first thing."

"You're scaring me."

"I'm sorry, but I can't talk right now. Please come see me right away. And call your sister."

She hung up the phone with a tightness in her guts she hadn't felt for a while. She rose and looked for the doctor, but he had shut the door behind him. She wouldn't get to say goodbye. Grabbing the one gym bag she'd brought with her, she walked out of the psychiatric wing and took the elevators down to the main floor.

3

When Samantha's plane touched down at Thurgood Marshal International Airport outside Baltimore, she had logged fourteen hours of flying time. As she walked into the terminal, her legs hurt, her back hurt, the atrocious food she had eaten sat in her belly like a lump of coal, and she had a migraine that was pounding ceaselessly against her skull.

Her car was back in Atlanta, so she waited on the curb outside for Duncan to pick her up. She felt bad that he had to come to the airport at five in the morning, but he said he was usually up jogging at that time anyway.

Before long, a gray Lincoln pulled to a stop in front of her, and she threw her gym bag into the backseat and climbed into the passenger seat. She kissed him and anticipated that, for a fraction of a second, he would hesitate to kiss her back since she'd just gotten back from an Ebola outbreak, but he didn't. Both of them worked with hot viruses, and he had grown accustomed to the roulette they played every day.

"How was Africa?"

"Hot. And the insects are the size of my head."

"Did you call your sister like I asked?"

"Yes, but she didn't answer. What's going on, Duncan?"

He was quiet as he pulled out of the airport and made his way to the interstate. "What did they tell you after the last outbreak of black pox?"

Images flooded Samantha's mind—patients turning to jelly and entire hospital staffs unwilling to treat them, a gymnasium full of patients because the hospitals didn't have enough room, and a man in her house who had nearly killed her.

She'd spent nearly a week in the hospital after the break-in. Two weeks after her release, she'd returned to her job and had been informed that the outbreak had been contained to Hawaii and South America.

"They told me it's over."

"Have you talked to your sister since she went to California?"

"No, she's been there a week. Her in-laws are there."

He paused. "Samantha, it was never contained."

"What do you mean?"

"It got to the mainland. California. We think some of the infected snuck onto flights out of Hawaii and landed at LAX. There're over a hundred reported cases. The problem is that they're spread throughout the state and are difficult to contain. Someone higher up than me made the call that California can't be contained."

"What does that mean?"

"It means they've been closing all the bridges and highways in and out. Shipping's stopped, and flights were grounded this morning. No travel to or from the state. They're imposing martial law today."

"You're exaggerating," she said.

"I'm not."

"They're going to violate the liberty of thirty-eight million people because of a hundred possibly infected?"

Duncan sped up the onramp onto the interstate. "Someone in the military's determined that this infection, Agent X, is deadly enough that it's the prime national security threat... at least for now."

Agent X. She'd thought she would likely never hear that again in that context. She knew that samples had been taken and stored in the Centers for Disease Control biosafety level four laboratories, which were the most secure laboratories in the world, where everything from Ebola and smallpox to a strain of airborne AIDS virus were contained and studied. The United States Army Medical Research Institute for Infectious Diseases was the only other laboratory stateside that could even compare.

"Why haven't I heard about it?"

"I only found out because we've been issued leave from all other projects to work on a vaccine. This is really top secret stuff. They're going to shut down the news stations and radio, even the internet. With the flip of a switch, they're going to shut down all information in an entire state." He shook his head. "The fact that they can even do that is what's most frightening for me. But anyway, they worked out some deal with the media outlets. You guys can stay on, but if you report anything about what's coming, you're done. They've got everything in place now, and they're going to make it official this morning. No one in or out, under penalty of imprisonment or death."

"Death?"

"That's what they said."

"It's too big a border to secure. They can't do it."

"You haven't worked in the military, Sam. You don't know how they think. They know they can't secure the whole border. They don't need to. Thomas Edison did an experiment with elephants. He chained them to the ground, and the elephants would try desperately to get away. He did it for a long time, and eventually, the elephants stopped trying to escape. Then Edison replaced the chain with a string. The elephants couldn't get away. They would feel the string and were paralyzed. They don't need to prevent everybody from escaping. They just need to make an example out of the first few people that do. Everyone else will be held in place by a string."

She sat quietly and processed that. All the pain and horror she had experienced during the past couple of months came flooding back to her, making her heart race. Short of breath, she had to close her eyes and take deep breaths to calm herself.

Agent X spread through even casual contact, and its incubation period was far shorter than even a normal strain of smallpox. Most viruses would have to flood the body to cause infection. The HIV virus, when passed through contact with an infected person, floods the new host's body with millions of viruses. Agent X, from everything they could tell, only needed one virus to enter the body to cause infection. The world, she was convinced, had never seen anything like it.

And the most frightening part was that they weren't sure where it had come from. They had found the index patient, or patients, in South America. They had been infected through a canister believed to have come from one of only two places in the world that still held diseases as deadly as smallpox: the United States and Russia. The thought that some rogue nation like Iran or North Korea had developed it as a weapon was much more terrifying.

She took out her cell phone and tried her sister again. The call went straight to voice mail.

4

After spending a day with Duncan, Samantha had to get back to
Atlanta. She'd filed her reports on the Ebola outbreak in Kinshasa
electronically, and she'd gotten a reply that the assistant director
wanted to meet with her in person to go over them.

Duncan drove her to the airport in the morning, where she kissed
him and said goodbye. He handed her something before she walked
through the metal detectors: a copy of Seneca's *On the Shortness of Life*.

"Now?" she said.

"Its subtitle is 'life is long if you know how to use it.' It's a book
about overcoming tragedy."

"Thanks. I don't know if I can concentrate enough to read,
though."

He hugged her, and she watched him as she went through the
metal detectors.

The flight didn't take long, and after landing and using the
bathroom, she retrieved her car from long-term parking. She put the
hundred-and-twelve-dollar parking fee on a government-issued
expense card.

Atlanta was warm but had a dry heat that didn't affect her. She rolled down her windows as she drove home and listened to an Enya station on Pandora.

When she arrived at her house, she was struck by how much she had actually missed it. It was really nothing more than a small brown-brick house with three bedrooms—one for her, one for her mother, and a guest bedroom that was never used—but it held a comfort she'd lacked growing up in apartments and condos in Southern California. Samantha went inside and heard someone in the kitchen.

She walked in to find her mother's nurse, Dana, cooking lunch.

"Back already?" she asked.

"I got done quicker than I thought. How is she?"

"Yesterday was bad. She didn't remember who I was and kept thinking I was a burglar. She tried to call the police."

"I'm so sorry, Dana."

"Hey, that's why you pay me the big bucks. She's much better today. She's watching her soaps if you want to go up."

Samantha dropped her gym bag by the closet and went upstairs to the bedrooms. She went into her mother's room and saw her lying on her back, staring blankly at the flat-screen television on the wall.

"How are you, Mom?"

"I didn't get my medication today. I need my medication for my flu."

Samantha sat next to her and gently brushed back her hair from her eyes. "You don't have the flu, Mom. But I'll check with Dana and make sure she gets your medication to you."

"I need my medication. It makes my throat feel better."

Samantha leaned down and kissed her forehead. She sat back up and held her mother's hand. Placing her back against the wall, she turned toward the television.

"So, what's going on in this episode?"

Within an hour, her mother was asleep. Samantha quietly rose, turned off the television, and left the room, shutting the door softly behind her. She went downstairs and found a note from Dana saying that lunch was prepared and in the fridge. Tuna fish sandwiches were wrapped in Saran Wrap, with small bags of chips placed next to them. She took hers and went out on the porch. Sitting down on her steps, she unwrapped her sandwich and took a bite, looking out over her neighborhood.

Her community was quiet, without any commotion in the short winters and few calls to the police in the long summers. The neighbors mostly kept to themselves, but they would invite her to summer barbeques and picnics, which she would always take her mother to. She tried to get her mother out as much as possible, but within the last year, that had been getting more difficult. The Alzheimer's was slowly sucking away the strong, confident person Samantha remembered as a child. It had set in early, while Samantha was still an undergrad at New York University.

Dates were the first to go; she'd started out missing birthdays and holidays. Those were followed by events. Her mother would frequently confuse something that happened to her sister with something that happened to her. Or something she saw on television would become an occurrence that had happened to her. At first, Samantha, her brother, and her sister were in denial. They attributed everything to the natural processes of aging. But when she forgot how to open a soda can, they knew something was wrong.

Samantha placed the sandwich down on her lap. She took out her cell and tried her sister, Jane, again, and then she called her sister's husband, Robert. Neither of them answered.

5

Samantha leapt out of the double-engine plane over a clearing outside of Atlanta. The chute was wrapped tightly around her, and the wind screamed in her ears. Her goggles were coming off, and she wished she'd adjusted them beforehand, but her mind had been elsewhere.

The ground in front of her looked like a patchwork of green and yellow squares stitched together with roads. Cars moved on the stitching like parasites, and she had hoped that she wouldn't see any. She'd wanted the flight to be her, the sky, and the ground.

On some jumps, she would imagine she didn't have a jumpsuit and that she was racing toward the ground to her death. She tried to imagine it so vividly that she would think the actual thoughts she might have before her death, rank the priorities in her life. It never happened. Something about the feel of the chute on her back never let her believe that she was actually going to die. But she had gotten that feeling in the biosafety level four laboratories more than once.

On one occasion, she had suited up and inflated the biohazard suit with positive pressure, letting the air from the hose push everything away from her body, then began running a routine test using samples of Lassa virus. By all accounts, Lassa hemorrhagic fever was one of the most dangerous diseases in the world.

The Lassa virus was known as an ambisense RNA virus, which meant it was a non-coding strand of RNA that attached to the main RNA code. It could cause RNA interference, blocking an expression of a gene. Experiments were being done on RNA interference, mimicking Lassa, to attempt to block the expression of genes that cause Down syndrome or even genetic heart conditions.

But Lassa's RNA interference had a much more sinister purpose: to stop the host's immune system from attacking the virus. It took over the immune system and used the body to reproduce the virus itself. In Sierra Leone, Samantha had seen what this did to a human body. Some of the symptoms were flu-like, such as headache and sore throat, and others were hemorrhagic, like bleeding from the eyes and genitals.

But she wasn't thinking of that when she had been handling the Lassa. She was thinking of her sister's upcoming wedding. Almost immediately after the experiments were complete, she noticed something on one of her gloves: a small tear.

The glove was thick double-stitched rubber. When she decontaminated, she pulled it off and checked the glove underneath—and spotted the same tear. Underneath that was the final layer, a thin sheet of latex. It was torn, as well.

Panicked, she quarantined herself in the laboratory. The CDC staff could do nothing but wait. They brought her meals, fluids, and books, but they had to wait for the incubation period to run its course. Once it had, a blood test showed she had not been infected.

Sitting in quarantine late at night, listening to the hum of the machines and the occasional plane flying low overhead, she questioned her life and her choices. She had reached decisions, but she couldn't remember them anymore. The terror of the moment was so strong that it overtook her reason, and her memory of the quarantine epiphanies faded every day that she was away from the laboratory.

Samantha pulled her ripcord later than she should have. The recoil jerked her up and sideways, and the sensation was jarring. She hit the ground hard and fell on her stomach as the chute collapsed around her like a deflating balloon.

She lay on the ground a long time, staring up at the sky through her rose-tinted goggles. Pulling them off her head, she took in a deep breath and then exhaled through her nose. She did this until some of the others who had jumped came up and asked if she was okay.

The jumps were relaxing and uplifting, but something was different this time. She couldn't exactly put her finger on it. But it seemed, almost, as if she were just going through the motions rather than experiencing the moment. The jump felt futile.

Whatever it was, she felt the same as she had before she'd jumped out of the plane.

After a change of clothing, she headed back into Atlanta, to Clifton Road, where the Centers for Disease Control and Prevention were headquartered.

Multiple buildings dotted the landscape, and most of them were rectangular and made of blue glass. A blue-and-white sign marked the white CDC emblem of a bird that she guessed was a hawk, but looked like a pigeon, and it sat at the forefront of the building.

After parking in her reserved stall, she tried her sister again and left a message, probably her fifth one, stating she was worried and would like a call back. Jane usually called her immediately. Going black for long periods of time was definitely out of character for her.

The metal detectors didn't buzz when Samantha passed security. She went up to her office on the fourth floor, which overlooked the grassy knoll across the street, and collapsed in her chair. Her hair was a mess, and she took out a hair elastic and pulled it back. Several papers were scattered over the desk and piled in two boxes in the corner. She pushed the papers aside and then turned on her Mac.

Her inbox said she had ninety-six unread e-mails. The number was so overwhelming that she turned on Pandora and sat there for a good fifteen minutes, unable to open even one. Then she stood up, stretched her arms above her head, sat back down, and began going through them. She scanned them quickly for anything important, anything about California. But she saw nothing relevant.

Someone knocked on her glass wall, and she glanced up and saw Frederick Hess, assistant director over Infectious Diseases, who waved to her. She waved back, and Fredrick came to the door. He leaned against it but didn't come in.

"How was it?" he said.

"Hot and terrifying. How was everything here?"

"Pretty much the same."

She grinned and leaned back in her chair. "The outbreak was contained. I think the final nineteen patients will probably pass, and that'll be it as long as the doctors from the WHO treat the bodies with care."

"Why wouldn't they?"

"Some of them are poorly trained on hot viruses. They're not common enough for someone from Thailand or Peru to deal with. They don't recognize how deadly they are." She paused. "There was a doctor there that became infected because he refused to leave patients untreated. I'd like to write an article about him. Maybe a blurb on the CDC website, if that's okay."

"He didn't run out the door like everyone else?"

"No. He knew he would probably die, and it was worth it for him."

"I didn't think doctors like that existed anymore. I'm on the admissions committee over at UMD medical school. You should see some of the reasons people put for wanting to become doctors. They think it's prestigious or they're going to make a lot of money. I tell them for the hours they're going to put in, they'd make more money managing a restaurant. And nothing's more prestigious than doing rounds, asking patients how much they pooped the night before."

"It has its moments. My uncle was a doctor as well, and he worked for Doctors Without Borders. I don't know of any other professions that let you travel to any country in the world and do good. I don't think lawyers and politicians can do that."

"Yeah, well, maybe actors adopting kids from countries nobody's ever heard of."

She hesitated. "Can I ask you something, Freddy?"

"Sure."

"Do you know anything about California?"

"Their taxes on small business is killing their economy."

"I meant have you heard anything about military involvement there?"

He glanced away. The movement was quick, but she caught it.

"It's classified, Sam."

"Classified? Since when is anything at the CDC classified?"

He stepped into her office and sat down across from her. "I know in medical school they trained us to question everything. To find every detail, even what someone's grandmother did for part-time work back in Uzbekistan when someone comes in with flu-like symptoms. But sometimes, as employees of the government, we have to stop questioning and just do what we're told."

"That sounds like you don't agree with what's about to happen."

"Doesn't matter what I think. I'm a cog in a wheel." He rose and started out of her office, turning back to her at the door. "I can tell you one thing, though. There's a Chinese curse that says, 'May you live in interesting times.' And this is definitely an interesting time."

6

Howie Burke finished shooting hoops at the park by his house, then lay on his back in the grass after chugging half a Gatorade. At forty-three, he thought he should feel younger than he did. He sat up and watched a few minutes of the other game going on, a five-on-five, and then made his way over to his jeep and headed back home.

The 405 was packed, and he occasionally thought it was quicker to drive to Las Vegas than to get around within LA. And it seemed even more crowded than a few years ago, as though a large migration into Los Angeles had happened. He wondered why anybody in their right mind would move there.

As a kid, he remembered clean parks and plenty of role models. An old man who'd lived in his apartment complex had been in the 101st Airborne, the division that had guarded the first black students to integrate into white schools. He remembered the man telling him stories of what people put those poor kids through. They hung black dolls with their genitals cut out from trees and threw bottles at their heads. The teachers wouldn't teach and forced them to sit in the back, away from the other students.

Howie also remembered a woman who had slept with Jack Kennedy, or so she'd claimed. She went into detail about it, and for a twelve-year-old, that moment was pretty gross but fascinating. In that little apartment complex, which was really his entire universe, he found all the villains and heroes he needed, and the outside world didn't seem to matter much. He had his friends, his family, and his neighbors. And every lesson of life he needed was learned there.

But the city had changed. The sense of community was done. He felt as if he could have lived in any apartment complex in Los Angeles, and no one would even have said two words to him if he didn't initiate the conversation. People were growing more distant from each other, and he wasn't sure why.

The drive to his house in Malibu took almost two and a half hours. His home was right on the beach. He parked in the driveway, unlocked the door, and turned off the alarm. The maids hadn't come yet that week, and a couple of beer bottles stood on the coffee table, and a few dishes sat in the sink, but other than that, no one seemed to live there.

The apartments he'd lived in growing up were always cluttered and messy, but he'd preferred a more sanitary environment ever since going out on his own at seventeen. His father, a raging alcoholic, hadn't noticed he was gone for months, and when he did finally raise himself out of his drunken haze enough to track Howie down, the only thing he did was ask for money. Howie gave him every cent he had on him and hadn't seen him since.

As he showered, he thought about where his dad might be. His mother had run off when he was a teenager. His father always told him she went to live on a ranch with her sister, but he'd later learned that was a lie. She was a secretary and had struck up a romance with someone at work. They fell in love, and she abandoned her son and husband for the beaches of Florida. When Howie's mother left, his father turned to the bottle. It began with beers at every meal and then turned to hard liquor and eventually to a Bloody Mary every morning for breakfast.

Howie didn't remember how old he'd been when he uttered those words that every child does—I won't be my parents. He was rich, sober, and full of confidence. Everything his father hadn't been. He dated beautiful women… but his relationship with his only daughter was no better than his relationship with his own father. Despite all his effort and all the different roads he'd taken, in a lot of ways, he had become his father. And a part of him hated himself for it.

Howie changed into a polo shirt and Dockers shorts, then put on Italian leather shoes and no socks. He went to his dresser and chose his watch, opting for the silver Rolex his ex-wife had bought him for his thirtieth birthday.

His ex-wife. Howie remembered that it was Friday and his one weekend a month to take his daughter, Jessica. He hadn't seen her for two months. Her mother and her mother's new husband, David, flew her around the world, took her on cruises, and kept her busy with private schools, cheerleading, and whatever else Jessica was into. David had two boys of his own, and they, from what Howie could tell, were as happy as could be.

He checked his cell phone and saw a text from his ex. *Where the hell are you????*

Replying that he would be right there, he headed to the fridge and got a bottle of cold water before dialing the girl he was supposed to see that night. He'd been dating Brandi off and on for over three months, which was a personal record since the divorce. It went to voice mail.

"Hey, Brandi. Um, listen, can't make it tonight. I've got my kid. I mean, my neighbor, Sandy, might be able to watch her, so I'll see if I can dump her off, but if Sandy's got plans, I'm kinda stuck. If you want to come over here and watch a movie or something, that's fine."

He hung up and headed out the door.

It was a forty-minute drive to Bel Air, and that was pushing it. Howie didn't want to rush, but the traffic was actually light compared to how it had been on his way home. Maybe it was just because it was three in the afternoon on a Friday. He called in to his company, an advertising firm, and asked his secretary to clear his schedule for Monday and Tuesday. He was going to take Brandi to Mexico as soon as he dropped Jessica back off at her mother's on Sunday.

His phone rang, and it was Brandi.

"Hey," he said.

"Hey. So no show? Sarah's one of my best friends, and this is her first gallery, Howie."

"I know. I'm sorry, but what do you want me to do? It's my weekend, and her mom said she had something planned that she couldn't get out of."

"This is disappointing. I'm very disappointed right now."

Howie thought she sounded like a four-year-old, and he wasn't sure if he found it cute or stomach-churningly disgusting. "I'm gonna make it up to you. How 'bout we go down to Cabo on Sunday?"

"Really? You can get out of work?"

"I own the place. What's the point of being the owner if you can't play hooky sometimes?"

"That sounds amazing. I've been itching to get out of the city. I have a shoot on Thursday, though."

"We'll be back before then. Pack that little outfit I really like. The one with the garters."

"Oh, I got something new for you. If you're a good boy."

He grinned. "Come over and watch a movie with us tonight."

"I can't. I have to be there for Sarah. She would have a panic attack if I wasn't."

"All right, fine," he said sluggishly. "I'll see you Sunday then."

"Okay, see you then."

The home in Bel Air was immaculate, and a gardener was tending to the rose bushes. Howie pressed on the horn rather than bothering to go to the door. No one came out at first, and he laid on it again. Eventually, the door opened, and his ex, Kaila, was there with ten-year-old Jessica. Kaila kissed her, said something to her, and then shut the door as Jessica walked across the lawn and got into the Jeep.

She sat in the passenger seat and didn't say anything.

"Hi to you, too," Howie said.

"Hi."

Howie pulled away from the curb and thought to himself that this was going to be a long weekend.

7

Howie stayed up as late as he could with his daughter. He tried speaking to her several times, asking about school, but she replied with one-word answers. They simply had nothing in common anymore other than blood.

Writing her off would have been easy. It *should* have been easy. But it wasn't. As he sat on the couch next to her, he looked at her profile and saw himself. On an almost-biochemical level, it seemed, he wanted her approval, and her admiration. But he couldn't have it, and that ate him up inside. He thought that maybe being a parent was just a means of punishment for the things you did to your parents and that he somehow deserved this for not being a good enough son.

"I'm gonna hit the sack," he said at around ten o'clock.

"Sure," she said, not taking her eyes off the television.

As he was heading upstairs, he heard her take out her cell phone and call someone. She spoke a few words softly that Howie couldn't hear, but he did make out two sentences.

"I don't like it here. I want to come home."

The words stung Howie more than he would've thought they would. He stood looking at her, and he pictured the young toddler that would run up to him, throw her arms around his neck, and kiss him hard. She would wrap her legs around his chest, and he would pick her up and pretend that she was falling. Then she would laugh her sweet laugh. Those times seemed like someone else's life.

He went upstairs and lay down in the dark after opening his balcony doors. A breeze was coming through, and he heard the ocean outside. A slit of moon hung in the black sky. He picked up his phone and texted Brandi.

How is it?

Everyone's pretentious and hitting on me. How's your daughter?

She hates me. I'll take the pretention any day.

Why don't you bring her down here?

Maybe another time.

Suit yourself. Can't wait for our trip. Bought something new ;)

That's—

Howie's phone suddenly stopped working and he couldn't send the text. He chalked it up to just one of those things that happens when technology is involved.

He reread her last text and grinned to himself. Then he placed the phone on the nightstand before taking in a deep breath and trying to relax enough to drift off to sleep. His eyes darted open, and he got up, got dressed, and went downstairs.

"Jessica, we're going somewhere."

"Where?"

"It's an art showing. You'll love it. Come on."

"Can't I just stay here?"

"No, come on, get on your shoes. Let's go."

Once they were out the door, Howie chose the convertible, thinking Jessica might enjoy the warm night air. Instead, she folded her arms and ducked low so that it didn't touch her.

"How's David?" he asked after several minutes of silence.

"Good."

"He treat you guys well?"

"Yeah. He takes us everywhere."

"Like where?"

"To the movies and to Angels games, surfing."

"He seems like a good guy."

"He is."

They arrived at the gallery on the edge of Malibu next to the Pacific Coast Highway, and he couldn't find parking, so they had to park at a restaurant. Walking back to the gallery, Howie tried to hold her hand to cross the street, but she didn't take it. He had forgotten that she was old enough to cross the street on her own.

The gallery was impressively decorated with garlands, and the dim lighting made nearly everyone appear more pleasing to the eye than they were. At least fifty people were perusing the artwork, the majority of which were photographs of things found on the street. At the entrance, a video of a subway car in New York was playing.

"What are we doing here?" she asked.

"I want you to meet someone."

Rounding a corner, Howie saw his girlfriend in the middle of a group of people wearing what appeared to be Chinese peasant clothing. They even had the communist hammer and sickle embroidered on their jackets. He walked up to her and waited until she noticed him.

"Hey," she said, smiling widely. She came over and kissed him on the cheek. "I thought you weren't coming?"

"Changed my mind. Thought it'd be best to get out of the house. This is Jessica."

Brandi smiled a wide, fake smile. "Hi. Your dad tells me you're staying with him this weekend?"

"Yup."

"Well, I'm glad you came down here. Do you like art, Jessica?"

"Yeah. I'll let you know when I see some."

Brandi's face looked as though someone had pissed in her drink, and though he tried not to, Howie couldn't help but grin.

"So show us around," he said.

"Sure." Brandi smiled, stepping between the two of them before taking Howie's arm.

For twenty minutes, they went from photograph to photograph to crappy painting and weird video. Howie tolerated it because of the simple fact that Brandi was a knockout, and it couldn't hurt him later to score points. But Jessica was rolling her eyes and grunting as if she were so frustrated she might have a meltdown.

At one point, they met the artist, a thin woman with a butch haircut and men's glasses, and Jessica asked her if she had dropped her camera in New York and then decided to keep the pictures.

After Brandi had shown them around, Howie could tell she wanted to mingle and introduce him to everybody, which he definitely was not in the mood for, so he said goodnight and forcefully took Jessica's hand as they walked outside.

"What's the matter with you?" he said. "She's a friend of mine."

"She's an idiot."

"She was polite to you, and you responded with nothing but rudeness. Who's the idiot?"

Jessica glanced away, her face contorting in anger. "Why do you even have me come over? You don't like it."

"Jessica," he said, kneeling down, "I love having you over."

"No you don't. I heard you talking to Mom once on the phone, and you told her there was no reason for me to come over."

He thought back and wondered if he'd really said it. "I didn't mean it that way."

"Let's just go."

When they got back to the house, she went straight to her bedroom that he kept for her and slammed the door. Howie felt as if he were living with her mother again, and it brought back bad memories.

He got a beer and then went out to the hot tub, where he stripped down to his boxers and got in. Leaning his head back against the side, he gazed at the stars and wondered if anybody was staring back at him.

He thought to the early years, the time when he and Kaila were dirt poor and happy. They were living in a studio apartment where the heater wouldn't turn off during the summers, so they had to soak towels in cold water and use them as blankets. The walls were so thin that he heard every one of his neighbors use the bathroom, burp, and even the crunch of their breakfast cereal when the TV wasn't on.

But he and Kaila had dreams. At night, they would lie awake and talk about all the things they would do once they made it. If they hung on until Howie graduated and got that first job, they would make it.

Eventually, they made it, but somewhere along the way, they lost each other. The divorce wasn't messy. Howie gave her everything she wanted. He didn't fight for custody, and he even sold his Porsche that he loved and gave the money to her. He wanted out and was willing to pay any price.

He wondered if he'd made a mistake. Maybe he should have brought Jessica to live with him? Her mother shipped her off to boarding school while she and David went off on vacations. She had two stepbrothers, but from what Kaila had told him, they were happy, but didn't really pay attention to Jessica. She was also hyper-intelligent and was in the gifted program at her school, which didn't help her win any friends. She was, as far as Howie could tell, almost entirely alone.

"Hey."

He looked over to see Sandy on the balcony next door. "Hey."

"I don't see you out here that much, drinking. Something happen?"

"That obvious, huh?"

She went inside and a moment later was out on the beach in front of his balcony. She climbed the steps and sat on the edge of the hot tub, a glass of wine in her hand. "Anything you want to talk about?"

"My daughter hates me. Same old."

"She doesn't hate you."

"How do you know?"

"I've talked to her. It's a defense mechanism. She thinks you don't care about her, and her defense is to convince herself she doesn't need you."

"I think she doesn't need me."

"Please. You're Daddy. Fathers are larger than life to their daughters."

He exhaled and took a sip of his beer. "What did you do tonight?"

"Just watched movies by myself. I was hoping you were home and we could watch one together."

"Now, what the hell is a girl like you doing home alone on a Friday night?"

She shrugged and placed her wine glass down. "Sitting in the hot tub with you."

Sandy slipped off the clothing she was wearing and stepped into the hot tub, then slid over to Howie. They kissed as some teenagers lit a bonfire farther down the beach.

8

General Kirk Lancaster walked down the Hall of Heroes at the Pentagon and stopped a moment to look out the windows. At five in the morning, he'd already been up for an hour. He couldn't sleep, and he'd thought about taking an Ambien but had heard they can cause psychotic episodes, so instead, he tried warm milk and chamber music. It didn't work.

He walked down to a large office, where he sat behind the desk and immediately spun the chair around to look out the windows at the hedges and the lawn. He didn't feel like staring at walls.

But the grass gave him an uneasy feeling, too. He had been at that desk on September 11th. He remembered running out of the building and seeing charred remains all over the lawn. He'd thought the entire country was under attack, and his first thought had been that Bin Laden was responsible. He had warned the CIA and the FBI for as long as he could remember, but no one took the threats as seriously as they should have. After all, so many people hated the United States that it was difficult to tell who would actually act.

"Sir."

Lancaster turned around and saw his assistant, Major Martin Boyle, salute.

"At ease. We're not on a battlefield, Marty."

"Yes, sir," he said as he sat down across from him.

"What is it?"

"Sir?"

"I assume you have something to say about this morning, so let's just hear it."

He swallowed. "I couldn't sleep last night."

"I couldn't either."

"We've closed off the major highways leaving the state, and all the flights out were cancelled about a week ago. Per your orders, we didn't cancel the flights going in."

"Good."

He hesitated. "I don't want to do this, Kirk. This is wrong. There're less than a hundred infected, and we know where they are. We could just quarantine them and—"

"Have you seen someone infected with Agent X, Marty?"

"No, sir. Just photos."

"I visited a military hospital up there, Loma Linda. They had a patient behind this huge transparent barrier. Like a bubble. And I went and pinned a Purple Heart to the bubble with tape. As I was looking in, he began to vomit. It wasn't food, though, it was blood… and organs. The vomit wouldn't stop, and it exploded out of him so violently, it looked like a grenade had gone off in there. And I saw his brains start coming out of his ears. The virus liquefies the organs, all of them, including the brain and skin. And all it would have taken for me to contract it is a single virus. Just one. If that barrier hadn't been there, he would have infected a dozen people, who would each infect a dozen more."

"But what we're doing to our own citizens, it's never been done before."

"You kiddin' me? Lincoln had Confederates arrested and held for years without ever seeing the inside of a courtroom. *Korematsu v. United States* was the case that decided that Japanese internment was justified. And guess what? It's still good law. It hasn't been overturned. In times of crisis, people always give up their freedoms, and they're happy to do it."

"This is different. This isn't targeting a group. This is indiscriminate. And we can't maintain order, General. We're talking about forty million people. We can't even scratch the surface."

"Use local law enforcement to help you. But, Marty, we're not letting this thing out. Not at any cost. We're talking about the end of our nation if this thing spreads. No more America. And if the U.S. falls, you bet your ass the rest of the world is going down with us. We have to do this."

"And you've cleared it with the Joint Chiefs and the president? The Justice Department?"

"Who do you think came up with the idea, Marty?"

They sat in silence a moment before Marty said, "Once we do this, there's no going back."

"I know." Lancaster paused. "Do it, Marty. Send the order now."

He rose. "Yes, sir." He took the emblems over his heart off his uniform and placed them on the desk. "It will be the last thing I do as Major under you, sir. I'm here voluntarily, and I quit."

Lancaster watched him walk out, and he leaned back in the chair. Marty was young and idealistic—two traits he himself might have had at some point. But if he ever did, they were so long gone that he didn't even remember them anymore. He cared only about pragmatic decisions and didn't understand those who took any other view.

He turned back to the window and stared at the lawn.

9

Samantha sat in her office around ten at night, scanning the news sites for any information about California, but she found nothing. She checked Facebook and Twitter and found only one relevant post under the hashtag #UFOSRREAL. A person was saying that she had seen a lot of activity at the military base near her house. They seemed to be preparing for war.

Sam stood and rolled her neck, then raised her arms over her head to stretch her shoulders. She walked to the window looking out over the parking lot and didn't see anyone out. Pacing her office, she bit her thumbnail.

Screw it, she thought. *I'm not doing any good here.*

After grabbing her jacket, she went out and got into her car. A bar where most of the people at the CDC hung out wasn't too far from there, and as she drove, she tried not to think about why her sister wasn't answering her cell phone.

She parked right out front and went in. The bar was packed with people shooting pool and throwing darts, and she saw a few of her colleagues at a table, nursing some beers. They waved to her, and she waved back but didn't feel like going over.

She chose a stool at the end of the bar, then ordered an orange soda with ice and sipped it quietly. She tried to resist, but eventually she gave in and texted her sister for the fiftieth time.

Where the hell are you?

No reply.

She tried her husband, and again, no reply.

Thinking of her sister's husband, Robert, brought back memories of when Sam was nearly married, to another medical student named Isaac Hinckley. He was a warm, intelligent boy, and they dated for so long, they'd grown comfortable together in that way that couples find the comfort better than anything else in the relationship. When he asked her to marry him, she said no. And to this day, she wasn't sure why. No was the first thing that had popped into her head, and she'd blurted it out. Even if she wanted to change her mind then, she couldn't. His heart was already broken, and he would have always known that her first answer was no.

Maybe she had turned him down because of her career or the fact that she was only twenty-two and wasn't ready to settle down. Or maybe her father loomed so large that anyone else seemed to fall short. He was a successful businessman, a rugged former boxer who dominated any room. Samantha idolized him, and she knew that his traits were what she was looking for in a husband, whether consciously or not. So far, in the halls of medical school and laboratories, she hadn't found them.

A man sat one stool away from her and ordered a beer. He turned to her and smiled. "Hi, I'm Brad."

"Sam. Nice to meet you."

"You, too. Haven't seen you here before."

"I'm not really a drinker."

"Who you texting?"

"Excuse me?"

"I saw you texting. Just wondering who."

"No offense, but I kind of came here to be alone."

"You picked a helluva place to be by yourself," he said.

He was right. Why would she come to a bar, of all places, to be alone? She finished her soda, then brushed past him on her way outside. A hiking trail wasn't far from here, and reaching the summit of a hill overlooking the city took only about fifteen minutes. After driving there, she was pleased to see there were no other people around.

The dirt on the path was smooth, and her hike was quick. She took out her mace and held it in her hand until she reached the summit, where she placed it in her pocket and sat down.

The lights of Atlanta twinkled, and a plane flying by overhead blinked rapidly from the cadre of illuminations along its body. Streetlamps looked like glimmering buttons in the dark, and farther up, past the mountains of steel and glass, were flashing radio towers. She wondered how much longer standard radio would exist with digital available.

The skyline was a mass of buildings pointing skyward, each lighted differently and with diverse company logos stamped over them. She noticed one for a bank, and she remembered that she needed to pay her credit card bill. She had called them earlier, but they'd said their system was down…

Her heart skipped a beat.

She pulled out her cell phone and looked up restaurants in Los Angeles. She called the first result in Google. She got a busy signal. She tried the second result and got the same. She looked up bars in San Francisco—all busy. A clothing store at a mall in Sacramento also had a busy signal, as did television stations, utility companies, and twenty-four-hour pharmacies. She looked up random people in the online phone directories, and their numbers went straight to voice mail. Calling another five, she got the same results each time.

Jane wasn't avoiding her.

10

When Ian's plane landed at LAX, he got off with the twenty-five other passengers. He guessed it would be one of the last flights into California.

His feet hit the terminal carpet at nearly seven o'clock in the evening West Coast time, and he checked his watch, then set it back an hour. As he walked through the terminal, past security, a man in a gray suit was walking toward him. The man placed a suitcase down about ten feet in front of him, and Ian picked it up and walked out of the airport.

He stood outside in the warm Los Angeles air, glancing over the palm trees, and was glad he wasn't in Chicago anymore. After growing up in Rio de Janeiro, he felt as though he were being strangled by the compacted cityscape of modern cities, and LA was no different. But at least in the oasis surrounding the airport, trees, open space, and a sweeping twilight sky existed.

He walked to the curb, where he saw a car with two men inside. He glanced inside, but walked past them. He walked past a minivan, then came to an Audi with a single female sitting in the driver's seat. The young blonde was trying to send a text. Looking in through the passenger-side window, he saw that the doors were unlocked. He opened the door and got into the passenger seat.

The girl looked at him, her face wrinkled in confusion, and then her eyes went wide as she saw the muzzle of the Smith & Wesson.

"If you scream or try and get out of the car," he said, "I'm going to shoot you in the face and then drive myself. Do you understand? Nod if you understand."

She nodded.

"Good. Now put it in drive and get on the freeway."

"Just take the car."

"I need a driver, not a car. If you do everything I say and you do it well, by tomorrow morning, I will be on a plane, and you can go back to your life." With his free hand, he pulled a wad of cash from his pocket. He counted out several hundred dollar bills and threw them on the center console. "And you'll make some money for your troubles."

She looked behind her. "Why do you need a driver?"

"I'll tell you when we move."

She put the car in drive and pulled away from the curb. Once they were out of the airport and winding their way to the 105, Ian lowered the weapon but left it on his lap, where she could see it.

"Where are we going?" she asked.

"You don't need to know that." Ian opened the suitcase and glanced inside. He closed and locked it again, then put it in the backseat. He opened the note app on his phone. Of the seven names he'd had two days ago, three were grayed out. That left four people, all with Los Angeles addresses. The name at the top of the list was Wendy Alvarez.

"What's your name?" he asked.

"Suzan."

"If I look at your driver license, is that the name I'm going to see?"

She hesitated. "No. It's Katherine."

"Katherine, I need your help for tonight. If something should happen to you, it interferes with my schedule, and I certainly don't want to interfere with my schedule. I have a flight scheduled for noon tomorrow, a flight where I'm the only passenger, and I intend to make that flight. So my inclination is to make sure you're safe. Do you understand?"

She nodded.

"I'm going to need you to say it."

"I understand."

"Good. So the only way you are going to get hurt tonight is if you change that inclination, which I'm hoping you won't. Take the third exit down from here."

Katherine took forty minutes to drive to Inglewood. Ian saw men on street corners throwing up gang signs at him, and groups of teenagers roamed the night as though they were in some post-apocalyptic capital.

"I was here once about ten years ago," he said. "It's gotten worse."

"What has?"

"The city. Maybe people." He looked to her and could tell she grew uncomfortable. "Who were you waiting for at the airport?"

"My dad. He's coming to visit me."

"He'll be fine. By the way, I can see that you're trying to hide your phone on the other side of your lap. Pick it up."

She glanced at him.

"It's all right. Pick it up."

She did.

"Call 9-1-1."

"No," she said.

"It's not a trick. Call 9-1-1. Tell them the make and model of your car, and give them a description of me. I'm serious. Do it."

"You'll hurt me."

"I give you my word. I will not hurt you. Call."

She looked down at the phone and held her thumb over the keypad for a moment before she dialed the number. It played an error message.

"Try your dad's cell," he said.

She called her father's cell and got a busy signal.

"It's not working," she said.

"No, it's not. So you can put the phone away. You don't need to hide it from me. Turn right up here."

She stopped at the intersection and glanced at a group of men on the corner and then at Ian.

"I wouldn't," Ian said. "They'll rob you, rape you, and leave you on the side of the street. I'm not going to do any of those things."

She swallowed and then turned into a residential neighborhood. The houses were worn down, and the dilapidated chain-link fences with missing sections did a poor job of protecting yellowed lawns. Some lawns were strewn with broken-down cars and parts and some, without any effort to hide it, simply had garbage thrown around. A few of the homes were kept up, though, and dogs were chained near the front doors.

"Stop here."

She pulled over to the curb and parked. They were in front of a white house with yellow trim that was lit up brightly by two small flood lamps.

"Get out and come with me."

They stepped out of the car. Ian glanced toward her and then back at the house. She looked down both sides of the street.

"It's difficult to tell, isn't it?" he said.

"What is?"

"How far you would get. I'm guessing to that corner right there before the slug exploded your skull."

"I'm not going to run."

"Good girl. Come on."

They walked up the driveway, to the front door. Ian knocked and heard voices inside. The door opened, revealing an elderly man.

"Can I help you?"

"Yes, I'm looking for Wendy."

"And who are you?"

"LAPD, sir. Is she here?"

"Lemme see a badge."

"Sure thing." Ian reached into his suit coat and came out with the pistol. He fired into the man's eye, and he collapsed without a peep. Katherine screamed, but Ian covered her mouth and dragged her into the house, then shut the door behind them. He heard footsteps in the kitchen, along with a woman's voice. "Robert, who's here at this—"

A woman came around the corner and stopped when she saw the gun in Ian's hand. He lifted it and fired three rounds into her chest. She flew against the refrigerator, leaving smears of blood on it as she slid down to the linoleum. He walked up to her while Katherine screamed behind him and fired another two into the top of her head.

"Let's go." He grabbed Katherine's arm and pulled her out of the house.

11

At midnight, Howie said goodnight to Sandy and then checked on his daughter. She was asleep in bed, with her earbuds still blaring music. He walked over and gently turned off the iPod and removed the earbuds. She stirred, and her hand went over his. Its softness reminded him of when she was much younger. When she was frightened, she would crawl in between him and her mother without saying a word, hoping they wouldn't wake up and kick her out to her own room.

Her sneaking into bed woke Howie every time, but he never said anything.

A pain shot through his gut, and he didn't know why. He left his hand there for a moment before pulling away. He went upstairs to his bedroom and showered to rinse off the hot-tub chlorine, then changed into gym shorts and a T-shirt.

He lay on top of the covers, staring at the ceiling a long time, and found himself drifting off to sleep, but the thought of his daughter continued to intrude on his peace. He exhaled and closed his eyes. Before long, his thoughts dimmed, and he fell into a dreamless sleep.

Howie wasn't sure what woke him, but he knew the sounds instantly once he was awake: men shouting and metal grinding on metal. He thought some neighbors were drunk and out causing trouble, but the noises were so loud, and there were so many men shouting, that unless the entire neighborhood was outside right then, it couldn't have been that.

He went downstairs, to the window in the living room. Looking out, he saw something he would never forget for the rest of his life.

Humvees were rolling down the street, interspersed with jeeps. Both were painted in camo browns and beige. Soldiers were there, too, or what he guessed were soldiers. They were knocking on every door, and if the door didn't open quickly enough, they kicked it down.

So many soldiers were crowded into the streets that it looked like a concert or a football game going on right outside his house. They were dragging people out in their pajamas, and some only had on underwear. One of his neighbors was hauled out of his house and thrown into a military truck.

Someone pounded on his front door. His heart seemed to stop, and he stared at the door as if it were something from another planet.

"National Guard, open the door!"

The door upstairs opened, and his daughter came down. "Who is that?"

Just as the words left her lips, the door exploded inward. His alarm went off as three National Guardsmen stormed in while Jessica was screaming. They grabbed him by the arms, but he didn't fight until one of them grabbed his daughter.

All three were wearing slim gas masks.

He pulled his arms away and swung at one, connecting with his jaw and sending him back. Then he felt an explosive force against the back of his head, and he was out.

The bouncing brought him around as the military truck rattled down the interstate. Howie came to and looked around. He was lying flat on his back. People were crammed into the truck on seats that lined the truck bed. Next to him, Jessica sat on Sandy's lap.

"Howie," Sandy said. She slipped Jessica off and bent over him. "Don't move. You took a nasty blow to the head."

"What the hell is going on?"

"Lay back. Take it easy. Let me look at your head." She reached back and then brought out her fingers. "It's not bleeding. How do you feel?"

His head pounded so hard it was giving him a migraine. Slowly, he sat up. The other people on the truck looked terrified and weren't talking. Behind them on the interstate was a line of Humvees, jeeps, and trucks. Several choppers, maybe as many as a dozen, flew above them.

"Sandy, what the hell is going on?"

"I don't know."

The ride was slow because the interstate was bumper to bumper with military vehicles. Civilian cars, which were empty, many of them with their doors open, were pulled over to the side of the road. He looked back to the cabin of the truck and saw a glass partition between him and the single guardsman who was driving.

Howie pounded on the glass, but the driver didn't turn around.

"Sit down," someone said. Howie turned to him. A middle-aged man in a tank top and boxer shorts caught his glare. "They'll put you out with tranqs if they see you getting upset. They did that to me. Sit down."

"Who are these people?"

"Army and National Guard. Now sit down before they tranq all of us."

Howie squeezed in between Sandy and the woman next to her. He was dizzy from the blow to his head, and when he glanced down, he noticed for the first time that he was in gym shorts.

"I was in bed," Sandy said, "and two men ran into my room. I started screaming, and they pulled me out of bed and threw a sweatshirt at me that was on the floor. They pulled me out and stuck me here. When I got in, Jessica was standing over you, and you were unconscious."

"Is it a terrorist attack?"

"I don't know. They won't tell us anything."

The road smoothed, and the truck turned off at an exit near the beach. It rode right out onto the sand and stopped. Several guardsmen came and unlatched the back, then shouted for them to get off. Slowly, they climbed out of the truck.

Howie put his arm around Jessica and whispered, "Stay behind me."

He climbed off and waited for his daughter. Two guardsmen were escorting them around the truck when Howie saw why they had brought them there.

Built right on the sand was a massive fence with barbed wire around the top. Two towers were arranged around it, and inside the perimeter, green canvas tents were set up down the beach as far as he could see.

This was a camp.

Someone pushed him from behind and told him to keep moving. He held tightly to Jessica as they walked with the crowds. The people were surprisingly docile. The fight in them had been spent. Now they were in unfamiliar territory and at the mercy of men with guns.

Beyond the gates, a guardsman with glasses stood at the front. He glanced up at them. "Men to the right. Women to the left."

"No, Howie, don't let me go there," Jessica said.

"Please," Howie said. "She's my daughter."

The man pushed his glasses up onto his forehead and looked them over. "Fine. But she's your responsibility. We will not be held for anything that happens to her."

"What's this all about?"

"Just keep moving."

Howie nodded, and they were led to the right, down a gated path that opened up onto a section of beach. He saw nothing but tents, cots, and men. Most of them were standing around talking, but a few had already lain down on the cots or gone inside the tents to sleep.

His daughter was holding his leg tightly, and he glanced down, then put his arm around her.

12

Samantha sat on top of that hill for several minutes. She could just go about her life as if nothing were wrong and wait for her sister to contact her. That would probably be best. She had her mother to look after, and the nurses could only do so much. But it wasn't like Jane to not contact her; whatever the government planned to do had already begun.

She bit her thumbnail as she stood up. She paced for a moment before pulling out her phone.

She tried to book a flight to LAX or John Wayne in Orange County, but no airline would allow her credit card payment to go through. She kept getting an error message and being redirected to the main site. Flights must have been cut off. She checked the clock on her phone, then dialed Duncan's number.

"Hey," he said, out of breath.

"Hey. What're you doing?"

"Elliptical. What's up?"

"Sorry. I know you hate people interrupting your workout."

"No biggie."

"So, you get access to military flights, don't you?"

"Sure, all military employees do."

"Could you book passage for someone else?"

"Only if I went with them. Why?" A pause. "Oh. Oh no, you're not thinking what I think you're thinking."

"She's in trouble, Duncan. I know it."

"Sam, it's not going to be like that. At least, I don't think. She should be fine. They just want to make sure people are safe. And besides, you haven't heard anything on the news yet, right?"

"It won't be on the news this time. In Oahu, they made it public, and the virus still made it to the mainland. They're going to keep it as quiet as possible."

"Well, I haven't heard anything, and there're at least twenty high-ranking army guys in my building."

"Duncan, I know she's in trouble."

"Well, look, we'll book a flight out there on Southwest or something, and—"

"You can't book a flight. You can't call anyone. All the communication lines are down."

"What? Hold on a sec." He paused again, much longer this time. "That's weird," he finally said when he got back on.

"I have to get out there."

"Why? What could you even do?"

"I don't know. I've dealt with this virus before, and—"

"And it almost got you killed."

Flashes entered her mind of a man inside her home—flashes of pain, motion, and blood. The trauma hadn't fully settled in yet, and it still stung as if it had happened just the day before. She suddenly grew uneasy, and her finger traced the outline of the mace in her pocket.

"I know. But I need to get out there."

Duncan mumbled something under his breath and then said, "Fine. I'll get us passage tomorrow on the next plane going out."

"I'd like to go tonight. Right now."

"Why?"

"It's going to be chaotic at first, and there won't be any precedents. It'd be good just in case we need to pull some strings to get back out."

"Get back out? What do you think's happening there, Sam?"

"I don't know. But I have a bad feeling about it."

13

Howie sat on a cot with his daughter lying down behind him. She was listening to her iPod and falling asleep. Kids seemed to have an amazing ability to sleep through almost anything. He glanced at her and then back out over the men. An uncomfortable thought came over him. She was the only female he'd seen on this side of the fence.

Guards walked the perimeter and were stationed on makeshift towers that seemed to be rising higher as time went on. But the crowds were so dense, they weren't able to pay attention to everything.

The man in the cot across from him was also sitting down and nervously rubbing his hands together. He smiled at Howie. "You ever been through something like this?"

"No," Howie said. "I don't even really know what *this* is."

"I was talkin' to some o' the other guys, and they said it had to do with the sickness."

"What sickness?"

"That flu or whatever that was in Hawaii some time back. You remember when they had to shut down the airport and all that?"

He did remember hearing something about it on NPR. But the public was so jumpy that anything unusual would set off a panic, so he hadn't paid attention to it. Avian flu, one of the most ridiculously docile viruses in history, had caused an enormous panic that triggered a drop in commodity and stock prices as people were anticipating Armageddon-like devastation. And of course, nothing happened. He had thought the virus they were reporting on in Hawaii had been something similar and that some doctor working for the government would come out and say it was nothing.

"I do remember that," he said. "What does this have to do with it?"

"It's here, man. At least, that's what they say. That it's on the mainland, and they're closin' off California."

"The entire state? That's impossible. The border's hundreds of miles long."

He shrugged. "I don't know, man. That's just what they sayin'."

Lighting was sparse, but out of nowhere, the entire beach was engulfed with illumination. Massive floodlights connected to generators turned on. The lighting was harsh and felt like the sun. A crowd entered both the men's and the women's sides, and couples spoke to each other through the chain-link fence, calming crying spouses and children.

"This is monstrous," Howie said. "They can't do this."

"Already did it, man. It's done." He put out his hand. "I'm Mike, by the way."

"Howie."

"Well, Howie, I wish I could say it was a pleasure to meet you, but this is about the craziest thing that's ever happened to me. Damn near shit my pants when them guardsmen broke inta my house."

Howie glanced around the space. He recognized only two ways to get out: the entrance he had come through and an entrance at the back that was sealed with a massive steel lock. Howie rose and said, "Mike, keep an eye on her for a second, would you?"

"No problem."

He walked past Mike and across the sand to the other entrance. A floodlight was directly on it, so he didn't go near. The lock was at least five inches thick. Howie glanced back to make sure Jessica was all right, and Mike was sitting in the sand next to her, anxiously glancing around at the other men who were pouring in.

"Keep moving."

Howie turned around and saw a guardsman staring at him through the fence. "Excuse me?"

"I said, keep moving. We don't want any guests near the entrances."

"Guests? Is that what we are? 'Cause I certainly don't feel like a guest."

A crowd of several men was gathering behind him, some shouting things. Others stood quietly by and eyed the guardsman. The guard seemed to notice, and he puffed out his chest, a steely resolve in his eyes.

"I said, get back," he shouted, pulling the semi-automatic rifle strapped to his back.

"What are you going to do? Shoot us?" Howie asked. "For what? Why are we even here?"

"I won't ask you again. Get back!"

"I want a lawyer," Howie said.

The men behind him were shouting, and several guardsmen had run over. The first one bit his lip, glanced around, and opened the door. When the lock was off, Howie rushed in, several guardsmen behind him. Howie thought he might be arrested, but the guardsman raised his rifle, and he realized that wasn't what was going on.

The butt of the rifle hit his nose so hard that he flew off his feet. Men were shouting, and fists were flying before he heard shots and screaming. As he tried to get up, a guardsman slammed his rifle into him, and he fell back to the sand, staring up at the moonlit sky through a fog.

14

Ian leaned the seat back in the Audi and glanced over at
Katherine. She had cried for nearly fifteen minutes straight and then
sobbed a few more before quieting down. When she was calm enough,
he asked, "You hungry?"

She looked at him in amazement and then back out at the road.

"Well, I'm hungry. You know anywhere good around here? I feel
like Mexican."

She was quiet a long while and then said, "Paiso is good."

"Paiso it is. Let's go."

She got off on the next exit, and they headed through a somewhat
rundown part of the city Ian wasn't familiar with. The addresses had
only street names instead of numbers, and most of the stores had bars
on the windows.

"How's a good girl like you know about this part of the city?"

"I used to work here."

"Doing what?"

"Delivering meals."

"To who?"

"Homeless youth."

He laughed. "Really? Wow, what an incredible waste of time."

"They're kids," she said quietly.

"Let me tell you something, Katherine. I've been everywhere in the world and met all kinds of people, and you know the one principle that applies to all of them? They are in their life exactly where their past thoughts have brought them. Our thoughts are what make us who we are. You keep thinking negative thoughts, and that's all you're going to bring into your life. Bailing out those that haven't mastered themselves doesn't help either person. It's actually an embarrassment to both."

"What about you?" she asked. "Did your thoughts bring you here?"

"They did," he said, looking out the window as they passed dimly lit liquor stores and fast-food restaurants with thick, bulletproof glass in the drive-throughs.

"So you thought about killing people?"

"No, I thought about efficiency. That's what I do. I'm an efficiency expert in an industry where that is sorely lacking."

After turning into a lot filled to the brim with cars, Katherine parked in back near the dumpsters and they walked to the entrance. A line stretched in front of the restaurant, and they were told it would be a half-hour wait. Ian checked his watch.

"Do you want to find somewhere else?" she said.

"No."

He took out a wad of hundred dollar bills and went to the hostess. He whispered, "Beauty is a terrible thing not to reward." Then he slipped her three hundred dollar bills. She took two menus and, without calling any names, sat them by the window.

"You paid three hundred dollars to eat here?" Katherine asked when the hostess had left.

"You can't put a price on quality," he said as he opened the menu and looked over the items.

After he ordered a chimichanga with spicy mole, he handed the menus to the waitress and asked Katherine, "You sure you don't want to eat anything?"

She shook her head.

Ian smiled at the waitress and told her, "Just me today."

When they were alone, Katherine looked around, and Ian noticed.

"You could scream your head off right now. But that wouldn't change anything."

"They would call the police."

"Eventually, yes, they would. But this is Los Angeles in a shitty part of the city. The police will take at least ten, maybe fifteen minutes to respond. And what do you think will happen in that ten or fifteen minutes?" He glanced over at a fat man in a suit who was accompanied by a woman dressed like a hooker. "You think he'll come to your rescue?" He looked at another young man of about twenty on a date. "Or how about him? Or maybe you think these poor waiters earning two bucks an hour plus tips are going to run over here and risk their lives for a customer?"

"Maybe."

He grinned, glancing back at a child at the table behind them. He leaned back in his chair, partially exposing the holster with the pistol inside. "I'll tell you exactly what would happen. Nothing. Not a single person in here would do anything once they saw this gun. I would pull it out, shoot you in the head, and then again in the heart to make sure you were dead. I would take the keys out of your pocket and then find someone else to drive me. Maybe the hostess."

She shook her head, her eyes on the table. "Why are you doing this to me?"

"I'm not doing it to you. You were brought here by your choices. The choices you've made in life brought you here, and the choices I made in life brought me to this side of the table."

"You're not making sense. You said our thoughts bring us where we are."

He smiled. "Thoughts make our choices, and our choices make our actions, which make our lives."

The food came out a short while later, and he ate with gusto, then chugged a full glass of water.

"You were absolutely right about that," he said. "That was delicious." He wiped his lips with a napkin. "So have you made your decision?"

"About what?"

"About whether you're going to scream or not."

She didn't say anything, and he rose from the table, leaving a hundred dollar bill next to the plate. He took her arm and dragged her out of the restaurant, and she didn't protest much.

Once they were on the road again, he pulled out his phone and checked the next name before he said, "Head to the 405. We got a thirty-minute drive ahead of us."

15

Dobbins Air Force Base was the closest air base to Samantha, and she sped down the interstate to get there in time for her flight. She wouldn't arrive in California until early the next morning. But she was too wired to sleep on the plane, so she'd brought her iPad, which had several movies on it she hadn't watched yet.

When she arrived, the flight wasn't scheduled to leave for another forty-five minutes, so she waited by the gate since they wouldn't let her in without proper clearance. Duncan had forced himself onto the flight and demanded that he go with her. She protested, saying he should be on the flight for purposes of getting her there and then fly right back after dropping her off. But he wouldn't take no for an answer, and she didn't fight hard. The truth was she could really use someone with her.

Within minutes of her arrival, Duncan appeared at the gate in a cab. He paid before getting out, then hugged and kissed her.

"You sure about this?" he asked by way of greeting.

"She's my only sister. And she's in trouble. I know it."

He nodded. "Okay. But we're going there as part of the military. I only got you clearance by saying the CDC needed access as part of a study I'm doing and that I couldn't do it without you. You cannot go anywhere without me. I'm serious, Sam. You have to stick by me once we're there."

"Why? What did they tell you was going on?"

"I'm not entirely clear on the details, but it sounds like they've shut the entire state down, and no one can leave. I don't know how they intend to enforce that, but that's their plan."

She shook her head. "I thought we were done with this. I thought the agent had died out in South America and Oahu."

"Nature doesn't know how to give up. But I think it's contained. Just under a hundred known infections, every one of them quarantined in a hospital. Hopefully, this will be over once no more cases appear." He looked at the guard at the gate and then back to Sam. "You certain?"

"Yes."

"Okay, let's go."

16

Dr. Aneil Deluge walked down the corridor of Saint Anthony's
Hospital in Napa, California. Under his arm, he carried a clipboard
with two intake sheets attached. He took the elevator to the quarantine
unit on the top floor, which was really nothing more than a portion of
that floor cut off from the rest.

The elevators dinged and opened, and he stepped off. The nurse
behind the desk smiled at him, and he smiled back without greeting
her. He walked the length of the corridor to a room separated from the
others. He looked in on the patient through a glass viewing window.

Candice Montgomery was a twenty-four-year-old student at Napa
Valley College. She was studying communications and had been a
cheerleader for the football team. Deluge hoped she had not been to a
game or practice before she'd been admitted to the hospital.

Her symptoms were, at first, indicative of the flu—fever, rashes,
headaches, and vomiting. But, in a progression so quick that Deluge
was left wondering if she'd been poisoned, her condition deteriorated.

First, she developed small pustules on her skin. Little bumps that looked like kernels of corn had popped up on her flesh. Then her eyes, throat, and nose became irritated and swollen. These symptoms were not entirely alarming to Deluge or the ER staff, but what happened next, they had never seen before.

She broke out in pustules so severely that they covered nearly ninety-five percent of her body. They even broke out inside her throat, on her tongue, and over her eyes. She had gone blind as the pustules ruptured the conjunctiva, iris, and pupil. Heavy scarring had occurred afterward, and he guessed she was permanently blind.

But a more alarming symptom had developed that morning. Her skin appeared to be black. Though full barrier nursing was in place and the risk of infection from an airborne pathogen was low, two nurses and a phlebotomist had turned down his requests that they tend to her. Since he had to suit up and withdraw the blood himself every time, running many tests was difficult. The pustules had made injections extremely painful for her, as well, and she would thrash about whenever the needle went into any part of her body.

The blackness underneath her skin had spread over her entire body, and she appeared as though she'd been charred. One nurse, brave enough to examine her, had revealed to him that Candice's membranes in her orifices were disintegrating. The soft tissue at the opening of her nose, anus, vagina, and eyes was slipping off her as if they had rotted away.

Candice had been at Saint Anthony's for eight days, and it only took one day of her symptomology for Deluge to notify the Centers for Disease Control. They had flown out, improved the barriers to prevent further infection, and then left. The man that had been sent, a doctor by the name of Cheney, told Deluge that she was too far gone for treatment and that they should keep her comfortable for the next few days. Nothing else could be done.

Blood tests had confirmed the presence of smallpox, but in a form the hematologist didn't recognize. The CDC had taken all her infected blood and the test results.

"There must be something we can do," Deluge had said to Cheney as he was preparing to leave.

"This pathogen is a hundred percent fatal."

"That's ridiculous. Nothing's a hundred percent fatal."

Cheney glanced at him and then handed him a sheet of paper. "Write down anyone that has interacted with her since she's been in the hospital. Then speak with her family and see if you can find out who she's interacted with in the five days before she was admitted here. If any of them are showing symptoms, they have to be admitted with a full barrier set up. If you have any concerns, here's the number to our local office. They'll send someone out to help you."

With that, Cheney left, leaving Deluge to wonder exactly what the hell he had on his hands.

Nancy Claiborne had worked at Saint Anthony's Hospital for thirteen years and loved every minute of it—even the horrible patients who yelled, threw up on her, and fought. They had once even wrestled a gang member to the ground because he was on PCP and had knocked the doctor out cold.

But her first shift in the quarantine unit was unnerving. Many of the nurses had refused to even go in, but she wasn't scared. She had dealt with the worst outbreak of flu she'd ever seen and had lived to tell the tale without a scratch.

She was in the locker room, changing into her scrubs. She put on her Crocs and then went out onto the floor. Walking to the elevator, she didn't really speak to anybody, which was unusual for her. But she wanted her concentration, and the best way to maintain it was to ignore others.

She stepped off on the top floor, and Dr. Deluge was standing in front of one of the patient's doors. As she came up next to him, she looked into Candice's room.

"How is she?"

"Stable, I suppose," he said. "Has she moved or talked?"

"Not since about three days ago."

"Any vomiting or bowel movements?"

"One bowel movement yesterday, but it was mostly blood." She shook her head. "Poor girl. She's my Mathew's age."

Deluge rubbed his temples with his thumb and middle finger. "I'm going home. I've worked a twenty-hour shift. Keep me apprised of any major updates."

"Sure."

As Deluge left, Nancy walked back to the nurse's station on the quarantined floor and relieved the lone nurse sitting there, surfing the internet. She stretched and then opened solitaire and began playing.

Around midnight, Nancy heard something on the monitor. She paused the video she was watching on YouTube and listened. It sounded like coughing. She rose and walked over to Candice's room to make sure she was all right. Glancing in, she nearly screamed.

Candice was covered in a thick black blood. The fluid was spurting out of her eyes, ears, and mouth. Nancy wouldn't say she was vomiting because the heaving reflex was absent. Her blood was just coming out of her body as if being pulled by gravity.

Nancy called the ER. "I need a crash cart and a doctor up here in quarantine right now!"

Unthinking, seeing only a young girl in pain, she ran in.

She pushed past the transparent barrier and turned Candice to her side. A metal bowl near her mouth caught most of the blood, but it was still coming out of her ears. Nancy grabbed a bedsheet and pressed it to her ear canals to try to slow the bleeding.

For a single moment, Candice stopped vomiting and sobbed. "Please help me," she cried.

Before Nancy could say anything, Candice convulsed violently and jerked onto her back on the bed. She vomited an explosive stream of blood that hit Nancy in the face. It was warm and smelled like foul steak.

Nancy panicked, turning Candice to her side again, allowing her to vomit into the bowl. But so much blood was coming that it filled the bowl and spilled onto the floor.

The door opened, and a crash team was there.

"No," someone shouted down the hall. One of the trauma doctors, Roger, ran over to the room and looked in. "Don't go in," he said. "Gear up first."

"There's no time," Nancy said.

She realized suddenly that the crash team was staring at her. She wondered why, until something wet dripped off her face and onto her hands. She touched her face and came away with the blackness that covered Candice. Until then, she hadn't registered that the blood on her face was hemorrhagic blood.

"Roger..."

"Get into the shower, now."

She walked to the bathroom in the corner of the room and washed her face and hands. She started slowly and used a little soap, and then rubbed her hands together furiously. She was using so much soap that the suds covered the sink. She scrubbed violently at her face, and after a short time the skin was raw and pink, and she was crying.

She screamed and ran out of the room. The crash team were in the supply closet where they kept the biohazard gear, and Roger yelled out to her, but she didn't hear. She was sprinting down the hall. She had to get out of there. The hospital walls were closing in around her, her heart was racing, and she couldn't breathe. Her chest was tight, and she worried she was having a heart attack.

The elevator took too long to arrive, so she sprinted down the stairs instead. Hysterical, she burst out onto the first floor and ran for the exit.

The sliding doors opened and another nurse, Lance Page, walked in. She tried to run past him, but ended up running into him, nearly knocking him off his feet, and their faces bumped.

"Nancy," he said as she stood and ran out the door. "Nancy, what's wrong?"

17

Lance Page felt hot. He was lying in his living room, watching television, and his eyelids were boiling. Sweat was pouring out of him, and he was shivering.

Someone knocked on his door. With great effort, he rose and answered it.

His supervisor, Michelle, was standing on the porch.

"Hi," she said.

"Hi."

"Sorry for popping in, but nobody's phones are working. We think there's a big outage or something."

"It's okay. What did you need, Michelle?"

"Hey, I know you just left, but you sure you can't come in? It's just that we can't get a hold of Nancy, either, and we're short two people. If you could come in, it would really help."

He swallowed, and his throat was tight. "Maybe half a shift."

"Half a shift would be an enormous help."

"Okay. Give me fifteen."

Lance put on his scrubs and sneakers, then headed out the door. He locked it behind him and then opened it again. He went to the fridge to get a soda and left again, heading toward Saint Anthony's, which wasn't more than a ten-minute walk from his house.

When he arrived, he went directly to the bathroom and used wet paper towels to mop his head, belly, and underarms. Then he clocked in and went to the nurse's station for assignments.

The day was grinding slowly through, and Lance only lasted a few hours before he felt like it was time to go. He checked the board. A twelve-year-old boy named Max White had come to the ER with stomach pains, and his mother was worried that he'd gotten food poisoning from uncooked meat at a barbeque.

Lance went in and did his best to smile.

"How are ya guys?" he said.

"He's started throwing up since we got here."

Lance bent over to take the boy's vitals, and a single drop of sweat rolled off his head and onto the boy. It struck his lips, and the boy wiped away the spatter with his arm without saying anything, but the mother said, "Excuse me, you dropped sweat on my son."

"Oh, I'm sorry. It's just really hot." He moved away from him. "I'll be right back." Lance went out to the shift leader and said, "I have to leave. I don't feel good at all, Michelle."

"No prob. I think the rush has died down. Thanks for coming out. You gonna be able to make it tomorrow?"

"It's my day off tomorrow."

"Oh, right. Okay, have a good one then."

"Thanks."

After getting home, Lance slept for four hours. He hoped a nap would make him feel better, but when he woke up, the fever was worse. He tried calling his girlfriend to come and spend the night, but he was too weak to walk over to his phone. His throat still felt tight, and he was having trouble breathing. His lips and even his eyes were dry from dehydration, and he knew he had to drink something but was too faint to get anything.

With all the strength he could force out of himself, he swung his legs over the edge of the bed and stood up. He got as far as the bathroom before he sat on the toilet to relieve himself, but something was wrong. He didn't have the normal sensation of release. It felt more loose and messy. He stood and looked down. The toilet water was completely dark; red-black streaks crossed the bowl.

Max White stood in his backyard with his two brothers and his two-year-old sister. He didn't feel well and hadn't for four days. He was hot and sweaty, and his mother kept giving him water, juice, and ice cream, but none of it made him feel better. He'd thrown up a couple of times, but that had stopped two days ago.

"Max, let's play," his brother Martin said. He flung a baseball at him, but Max couldn't lift his arm in time to catch it. It struck him on the side of the head, and he fell back and lay on the grass. He wanted to lie in bed. It had been his mother's idea to come out to get some air and sunshine. He sat up.

"You all right?" Martin asked.

Max stood. His throat was on fire, and he took the soda Martin was holding. He drank down a few gulps before handing it back to him. "I don't feel good."

"Oh my gosh!" Martin screamed. "Mom!"

Rebecca White came out of the house and saw Max collapsed on the grass. Martin was standing next to him. Her eldest son and young daughter were playing on the other side of the yard.

"Martin, what's going on? What did you do to your brother?"

Martin was trembling. As she came upon Max, she screamed.

Blood was gushing out of his eyes and nose. He opened his mouth to talk, and a torrent of blood spewed out over Martin and the lawn. Max tried to cry, but vomited instead. Rebecca scooped up her son and ran to the car to drive him to the hospital, Max spitting up onto her chest and neck as she ran.

18

Howie woke with a banging in his head and was sitting up before he even knew where he was. He always thought that people who'd been knocked out woke up slowly, like they did in the movies. He'd thought his vision would be blurry at first and then he would hear things and slowly come to. But that was not what happened.

He was lost in a sea of darkness and barely aware of himself, and then, out of nowhere, he was back. He jumped up so violently that he tweaked his neck. He was leaning against a chain-link fence, but the area he was in was much smaller than what he remembered. Around him were four other men and only three cots.

"You all right?" one of them said, a man in a tank top, whose arms were covered with tattoos.

"That's the second time that's happened today." Howie groaned, twisting his neck. "Where am I?"

He shrugged. "Your guess is as good as mine. We still in LA, though, but we ain't near no beach."

Howie looked around. He was surrounded by trees, and a single guardsman sat at a table, with his feet up.

"What is this place?"

"Told you, man, we don't know nothin'. They ain't sayin' shit."

Howie rose to his feet. He was dizzy and touched his face, feeling the stickiness of dried blood. "My daughter," he said. "I left my daughter at that place by herself."

"Take it up with him," he said, pointing with his chin to the guardsman. "But he ain't in a talkin' mood. That one there tried to talk to him, and the soldier damn near shot him. If I were you, I'd keep quiet right now. Everyone's on edge."

Howie shook his head. "This is America," he said, a hint of panic in his voice. "This is fucking America. They can't do this."

"Hey, man, you preachin' to the choir. I lived off the grid in Montana lotta years. Then I come here for work and ain't here but six months, and now I'm in a cage. But shit, how'd people like you not see this comin'? All them phone records and e-mails the government was collectin'. Our passwords, bank info, what movies and books we liked. What did you think they was gonna use all that for? This is about control, man. That's the only thing government can do. Control. Ain't got no other purpose. It's blind to everything else."

Howie leaned back against the fence, putting his hands to his head. He took a deep breath to calm himself, but it didn't help. "There's gotta be a way out of here. I have to get back to my daughter."

He shrugged. "Wish I could help, man. But the only door's got a lock on it, and that muthafucker right there's got the key. How you think we get it?"

Howie glanced at the guardsman and then back to the man with the tattoos. The chain-link fence was a military brand and the holes were much larger than standard. "Just do what I say, and follow my lead." He shouted to the guardsman, "Hey, hey, please come here. Hey!"

The guardsman appeared annoyed. He was playing on a cell phone, which he put down, and stood up. Howie saw the outline of the rifle slung over his shoulder. The guardsman came to within a couple of feet of the fence.

"What do you want?" he asked.

"I need my heart medication. I have heart disease, and if I don't get my glycerin, I'll have a heart attack."

"There's nothing I can do about that."

"Wait, don't leave. Please. Look, give me a pen and paper, and I'll write down my address and the medications I need. Maybe you could give it to someone to get for me." The guardsman didn't move. "I will die in here. How do you think your superiors will feel when my family files a lawsuit against you and the army for refusing to give me my medication? And there's money at my house. In a drawer in the kitchen. Cash. It's yours if you get my medication."

The guard watched him a moment and then walked closer. He took out his phone and opened his text messages. "I'll send a text to someone that can maybe go pick it up. Where do you—"

Howie reached through the fence, tearing up his hand and wrist as it scraped through, and grabbed the man's shirt, pulling him to the fence. The man behind him, without even a hint from Howie, jumped up, took the guardsman's fingers, and pulled his arm through up to the elbow, gluing him in place. The guardsman went for the pistol in his waistband, and Howie grabbed his wrist.

The barrel was pointed toward Howie's stomach. He pushed with everything he had until the man with the tattoos bent down and bit into the guardsman's hand bad enough to draw blood. The guardsman screamed, and Howie ripped the pistol away from him and stuck it into his ribs.

"Where's the keys?" the man with the tattoos yelled.

"In my pocket. On my shirt. In the fucking shirt."

The man reached through the fence, into the guard's shirt, and pulled out the keys. He whistled and tossed them to another man by the door. The other man reached through the gate to the lock and inserted several keys before finding the right one. Then the lock clicked open.

"Kill him," the man with the tattoos said.

Howie glared at him. "I'm not going to kill him."

"Let me do it then."

"No, he's an American soldier."

The man laughed. "In case you ain't noticed, we at war now, man. Gimme the gun."

Howie twisted the gun so that he could pull the grip in first and then angled it to pull it through.

"Give it to me."

Howie felt the weight of the gun in his hands. He had never owned or even shot a gun before.

"No, we're not killing him. He's just doing his job."

"Ain't that the truth. And his job is lockin' us in cages, man. Gimme the fuckin' gun."

"No."

The man smiled. Before Howie could even blink, the other man struck him in the face with an elbow, making him see sparkling lights, before kicking Howie in the chest, throwing him back into the fence. The man grabbed him and proceeded to bash his fist into his face several times before flinging him to the ground and kicking him so hard in the face that Howie thought he'd shattered his cheekbones. He tasted blood that dribbled out of his mouth and onto his neck.

The man pointed the pistol at the guard, who tried to scream but was cut off by the round that entered his mouth and blew out the back of his head. He collapsed backward, and the man turned and placed the muzzle of the gun against Howie's temple.

"Please," Howie slurred through the blood, "Please. I have a daughter."

The man smiled, tucking the gun away into his waistband. "She ain't your daughter no more, man. She government property now."

The men fled the cage, leaving Howie bleeding and in pain on the soft ground, the corpse of the guardsman next to him like a bad dream.

19

Ian glanced at her as she drove. She had calmed down a little, and
he didn't get the impression she was constantly searching for an escape,
although that should have been her only thought. She had seen his
face. She couldn't expect to survive. Then again, for some reason, he
kind of liked her.

"What's your name?" she said.

"My name?"

"Yeah. You asked me my name. What's your name?"

"Ian."

"If I looked at your driver license, is that the name I'd see?" she
said.

He grinned. "No. It's not. But it might as well be."

"So what happens now?" she asked.

"You drive me around, and you drive me around some more.
Then I let you go."

"That's it?"

"That's it." He looked out the window at the commercial area they were in. Some of the office buildings bordered on being qualified as skyscrapers. "You see that building there? The tall one with the blue lighting?"

"Yeah."

"Stop there."

As the car pulled to a stop in front, he got out first and then waited for her by the hood of the car. She paused a moment in front of the open door. *This is it,* he thought. She was going to make a run for it. He slipped his hand into his suit coat. Her eyes went wide, then she shut the door and came to him.

He took her arm and led her into the building. The glass building was fifteen stories and had a nice atrium with a security guard. Gardenias and petunias in fanciful vases sat on glass and wood tables. He smiled at the security guard and squeezed Katherine's arm, prompting her to smile and say hello. *Smart girl,* he thought.

He pushed the button on the elevator, and the security guard rose from his table and started over.

"Oh," she said, "My uncle's working late. We're trying to convince him to come eat with us."

"Who's your uncle?" the guard said.

"Robert with Gem Mortgage. They're on the seventh floor."

The guard studied them. He rolled his eyes and returned to his desk, to whatever website he'd been looking at. When the elevator opened, they stepped in and didn't speak until it closed again.

"How did you know that man worked here?" Ian said.

"I looked at the directory when we walked past it."

"Hmm," he said, impressed. "You saved that security guard's life."

"Rather than take five seconds and spare his life, you just wanted to kill him? Why would you do that? Don't you care if he has a family? What if he has kids?"

"They might be better off growing up without a father."

"Is that what happened to you?"

"No." He checked the magazine in his firearm before holstering it again. "My father was a raging alcoholic that lived to a ripe old age. Until I was sixteen years old, he would beat me and my mother a few times a week so badly we'd have to go to the emergency room. We couldn't keep going to the same one because the cops would get involved, so eventually, we were driving two and a half hours to go to a hospital or clinic that hadn't seen us before." He glanced at her. "So like I said, they might be better off."

She stared at him, holding his gaze. "You're lying."

He chuckled. "My parents live in Iowa and couldn't be a nicer couple."

"Do they know what…"

"What I do for a living? They think I'm some mid-level bureaucrat."

She kept her eyes forward, on the doors, as the numbers on the dial above them slowly increased. She didn't say anything until the elevator had stopped and the doors opened. When they stepped off, she said, "You're going to kill me, aren't you?"

"Only if you don't do as I say."

"No, you're going to kill me anyway."

"Why do you say that?"

"Because you don't have a soul."

He stopped and looked at her. Taking up her arm again, he marched her forward.

The law firm's name was emblazoned across double doors with frosted glass. The secretary had already gone home for the night, but a few people still remained, grinding away the nighttime hours. He opened the door and pulled Katherine through with him.

They walked past two people talking near the front desk. Ian tried checking the names on the doors but found there weren't any, which was symptomatic of somewhere with high turnover. One man was sitting at his desk, drafting a document.

"Excuse me," Ian said. "Where's Mandy Hatcher's office?"

"Um, three doors to the left, down the hall."

"Thanks."

"Who are you guys again?"

Ian ignored him and walked to the office. He opened the door and pulled out his pistol. The office was empty. He went back to the lawyer he'd spoken to before.

"She's not in. Do you know where she is, by chance? I'm her brother-in-law."

"Oh, you're Tommy. Nice to finally meet you."

"You too. Mandy talks about me, huh?"

"She told us about Ice Cybernetics and how you started it with Kickstarter money and all that. Very cool. Hey, I need some advice on something. If Kickstarter offers me money and then I change my mind, and I—"

"No offense, but do you have any idea where Mandy is? Sorry, it's just I want to grab something to eat with her and catch up before I have to leave in the morning. She doesn't know I'm here."

"Oh. Well, whenever we have to work late, her and some of the girls go down to Ah Shucks. It's a bar and grill next door."

"Right, I saw it coming in. Thanks for your help."

"Hold on," he said, standing and minimizing the browsers on his desktop. "I'll come with. I could use a drink."

"Sure," Ian said.

"No," Katherine blurted out. "No, I don't really... I don't know. I just want to have a quiet dinner with Mandy."

"Um, okay."

"Okay," she said.

Ian walked her out and back to the elevator. "If you ever speak up again without my permission—"

"I saved you the hassle of having to kill someone in a public place. So you're welcome."

Ian glanced at her and then stared forward again, until they were off the elevators. They went outside, where he spotted the bar's white canopy over a green-striped door.

Ian stepped out front as two women were walking out. He recognized one of them and quickly spun Katherine around and put his arms over her waist, pretending to be whispering to her. He slowly took out his phone and checked Mandy's photo. The picture was perhaps a few months old, but that was the same woman.

As the women were walking down the sidewalk, two men ran up from behind. One of them smashed what looked like a small bat into the head of the other woman and then into Mandy's jaw. They picked up Mandy and dragged her to a van parked at the curb.

Ian laughed.

"Wow, today is not her day."

Katherine wasn't even smiling.

"Looks like someone else had the same idea," he said.

Ian casually strode up to the two men. One had opened the back doors to the van, and the other was holding Mandy, who was unconscious. On the inside of the van were shackles and chains.

Ian grabbed the man's wrist and jerked it away from his body before spinning it toward him and then snapping it in a direction it wasn't supposed to go. The man screamed, and Ian thrust the tips of his fingers into the man's eye, popping it out of the socket. He bashed his fist into the man's sternum which knocked him back.

The other one swung at him with the bat. Ian grabbed it with both hands on the downward motion and slammed it back into his face. He kicked down into the man's shin and then his knee before twisting behind him and smashing his face through the van door's window. He opened the door all the way, almost gingerly placed the man's head inside the van, and then slammed the door, again and again and again, until blood had spattered inside the van and his brains were laying there like jelly.

"Hmm," Ian said. He pulled out the pistol and fired into the exposed brain. "Never done that before."

Mandy was groaning on the warm cement. Ian pointed his pistol.

"No!" Katherine shouted. "Please don't!"

"As you wish." He tucked away the pistol, and relief washed over her face. In one violent motion, he knelt and spun Mandy's head almost all the way around and then twisted it backward, separating the spine from the body at C2, the spine's weakest point. Katherine was screaming as he ran to her, grabbed her, and pulled her back to the car.

20

Samantha watched the twinkling lights of the Midwest below her. In the dark, inside the gray military plane, she couldn't really see that she was being held aloft by a machine, and she appeared almost to be floating above the surface of the earth.

Duncan sat next to her and listened to an audiobook on his phone. She watched him for a moment, thinking back to the proposal she had received in medical school, and wondered what her answer would have been if Duncan had been the one making it.

"I never get over planes," he said, removing his earbuds. "That, with the power of our minds, we've been able to lift off the ground and sit back and fly. It's an incredible accomplishment of the human mind, and no one appreciates it. They just complain when their flight is ten minutes late."

"I think people have always been that way."

He took a sports drink out of his gym bag at his feet and took a long drink before offering it to her. She took a few sips, then pulled out some aspirin and took one with a drink before handing the bottle back to him.

"How ya doing with everything?" he said.

"Good as can be."

"Do you still get panic attacks sometimes?"

"They've been reduced. But I heard a loud crash the other day, just my mom dropping something, and it gave me one. Any time I'm startled. And I can't go to bed without checking all the doors twenty times." She glanced out the window again. "I've been seeing a psychiatrist."

"Why didn't you tell me?"

"I didn't know how you would react."

"Sam, someone tried to kill you. Not to mention everything that happened in South America and Oahu. You've been through some serious trauma. I would be surprised if you didn't go to therapy. I went to a shrink for about five years a little bit ago."

"For what?"

"Depression. It runs in my family. My grandfather and biological mother both committed suicide."

"I didn't know that."

"It's not something I talk about much. But anyway, I'm terrified of that, and so when I get even a hint of the blues coming on, I go to a shrink. Sometimes, talking is enough, but occasionally, I need meds."

She placed her hand over his. "I'm glad you told me."

He smiled awkwardly and took a drink of his bottle.

When her plane landed at Los Angeles Air Force Base, Samantha had been on the plane for three and a half hours, which was actually less time than she would have spent on a commercial flight. She and Duncan stepped onto the tarmac, and a warm gust of wind hit her. The sensation was both pleasing and ominous. The last time she was in this city, she was nearly killed.

A national guardsman in a jeep saluted Duncan, not knowing he was a civilian scientist working for the army, and threw their bags in the jeep.

"Sir, I'll be taking you into the medical station."

Sam climbed into the backseat, allowing Duncan the passenger, then the jeep started and peeled out from the tarmac, heading toward the city.

"Who's in charge of the medical station?" Duncan asked.

"Lieutenant General Olsen, sir."

Samantha asked, "Clyde Olsen?"

"Yes, ma'am."

She thought back to the time she had met Dr. Clyde Olsen. He had joined the army to pay for medical school and had decided that a career in the military suited his temperament better than one in medicine. "Medicine is guesswork," he told her once, "but the military requires no guesswork. You do what your superiors tell you, and your underlings do what you tell them."

The last time she had seen him was at a conference in London. He had gotten drunk afterward and invited her to his room, but she turned him down. So he'd picked up one of the other doctors at the conference, and they were arrested for having sex in the hotel pool after hours.

As the driver hopped on the interstate, she sensed something extraordinarily wrong. Not a single car was on the road. She saw no motorcycles or buses—nothing but military vehicles, particularly large trucks with people crammed in back.

"What's going on?" she asked.

The driver glanced at her and then back to the road. "You'll have to take that up with General Olsen, ma'am."

As they got onto the 405, she still didn't see any cars, but did spot at least five UH-60 Blackhawk helicopters. When they exited the highway, she knew what had happened inside the homes and stores, and it made her stomach churn.

No people were there. Doors on homes were left open. Stores had lights on, but no one was inside. The city was empty.

"Duncan—"

"I know," he said, reading her thoughts.

21

Howie stood up. Pain flowed through him as though someone had hooked up a hose of it to his head and let it drizzle down into his body. One of his teeth was loose, and when he tugged on it softly, it came out. He spit out the warm blood that flowed from the hole in his mouth. He walked out of the cage and around the guardsman heaped on the ground. He knelt down and held his breath, not knowing if a body could smell so quickly. He had never seen a dead body up close before.

The only one he could even think of was his grandfather, who had passed away a day short of his seventy-third birthday. He'd gone to the wake, but he wouldn't go near the casket. He stood on the other side of the room, catching only glances of the pale, mannequin-like face that jutted out of the gleaming box.

His parents kept telling him to go say goodbye, but he knew, even at ten, that there was nothing there to say goodbye to anymore.

Ten.

He thought of Jessica. Reaching into the guardsman's pockets, he searched for anything he could use—keys, money, cards. But the only two useful things he found were a knife and some matches. The other men had taken the rifle.

He tucked the knife, a good military-issue knife with a serrated edge, into his waistband and put the matches in his pocket. He glanced around. He had thought that fifty other guardsmen would run up once they heard the gunshot, but none came. Why would they only have one person guarding everyone in that cage?

He walked through the thicket of trees and soon came to a hill. He climbed it, each step more painful than the next, and had to stop to check his ribs. Placing his fingers over each one, he pushed on them to see how much pain it caused. When he got to the third one down on his right side, the pain nearly toppled him. The rib was fractured, or at least bruised—it had to be. But he wasn't sure what he could do about it, so he kept walking.

As he came to the summit of the hill, Los Angeles was below him. But it didn't look like the Los Angeles he'd grown up in. Lights were on, but far fewer than any other night. At least half the city had gone dark. And over the city were the blinking luminosities of military planes and choppers coming and going.

He tried to orient himself by searching for landmarks, but it was too dark to see much. Glancing behind him, he was surprised to see the Hollywood sign. Dilapidated and small, its reputation gave it gargantuan proportions and a mythical ambience. But, like the city, it was an illusion, and just underneath the glossy exterior lay mold and rust.

I'm in the Hollywood Hills, he thought. *How long was I out?*

It didn't matter. He had to get back to Malibu. Jessica was alone.

He turned down the hill. Hearing voices, he stopped and ducked low. He slowly crawled near the trees and peeked out. He saw another cage like the one he'd been in, and another guard sat at a table in front of it. Farther out, maybe two hundred yards, was another cage and another guard. A little farther than that, though hazy in his vision, was yet another one. That's why each cage had only one guard: they didn't have enough soldiers to spare more than one.

He slid back into the bushes and then went up the hill a ways, careful to stay underneath the trees and away from the road. The choppers overhead were loud, and they had spotlights, but they didn't fly over him. He kept walking, passing mansions on the way down, and realized he was still in gym shorts without shoes, and his feet were cut. In this situation, clothes didn't matter one bit, but he needed shoes.

Palm trees adorned the massive driveway of a particularly beautiful home with a white façade and red Spanish tile roof, just up ahead. Howie crouched and was silent for a moment to make sure he didn't hear any voices. Then he went up to the house.

The front door was wide open, so he walked inside.

The home was immaculately decorated with imported rugs, white marble busts, and a fountain in the center of the front room. Under normal circumstances, he would have been impressed and even a little jealous, but now the ostentation seemed utterly meaningless. *What a waste,* he thought.

He climbed a winding staircase to the second floor and located the master bedroom. Going to the closet, he found several suits on one side and women's clothing on the other. The suits were too big for him, but he went through the casual clothes at the end and found some jeans and a silk tight-fitting shirt. He put them on and then checked the shoes. They were close enough, perhaps a size bigger than he needed.

His feet were bleeding and black. He went to the tub and washed them.

He slipped on dress socks and then the shoes. As he went back downstairs, he paused on the stairs, wondering if the house's owners had guns. He ransacked the bedrooms and didn't find anything. Weaponry wasn't hidden downstairs, either. He was about to walk to the fridge before leaving, when he heard something behind him.

He froze, his fingers searching for the knife he'd tucked away. Slowly, he turned around.

A black Rottweiler with inch-long teeth was growling at him. The dog had an expensive collar, but other than that, it appeared to be a wild jungle beast.

"Easy," Howie said. "Easy."

The dog was sizing him up but had determined he was not a threat. Howie saw it in his eyes. He grabbed the knife and pulled it out, holding it tightly.

He turned and sprinted as barking filled the air, along with a cacophony of snarls, growls, and paws running on hardwood floors. Howie dashed into the kitchen, where gleaming pots and pans hung from the ceiling over an island cabinet. He jumped onto the island as the dog lunged for him and bit into his shoe, ripping it off.

Howie climbed up while the dog was trying to take a piece of him, leaping into the air and snapping in front of his face. He stood up as the dog got both front legs up onto the island, but it was too large to pull himself up.

Howie swiped down with the blade, and the dog yelped as the knife cut across its nose. But it only served to enrage him. It jumped again, and Howie screamed as it got over the island and fell into him with all its weight. He flew backward, hitting his head on a cupboard as he landed on the floor with a crash and several pots and pans fell over the island.

The dog bit into his arm, and he screamed. With his other arm, he thrust the knife as hard as he could into the dog's neck. But it didn't let go. He thrust again, and again, and again. The blood sprayed over the kitchen as if it were being shot from a hose, and Howie kept thinking to himself that he couldn't believe how much blood was coming out of this animal.

Finally, after coating the kitchen in blood, the dog stopped moving. But its teeth were embedded into his arm, and he couldn't pull away. He was out of breath and had to lie there, with the weight of the animal on top of him. When he had caught his breath, he reached into the dog's mouth and lifted its upper jaw, which crinkled like paper. Pulling his arm out, he rolled the dog over and lay there another moment, staring at the ceiling and panting.

I could leave right now. Nevada wasn't too far. The trip might take him a few days, depending on what kind of transportation he had, but he could do it. Jessica didn't want him near her anyway. She'd chosen to live with her mother and only came around when she was forced.

He took a deep breath, and stood. *She's my daughter,* he thought. *She's my daughter.*

As he was leaving the house, he noticed a small rack in the kitchen, containing several sets of keys. He took them all and ran around, checking doors until he came to the garage. Five cars filled the space. He opened the garage's exterior door and walked to the car at the end: a yellow Ferrari that would stand out far too much. Next to that was a black Mercedes. He stood and admired it a moment before climbing in, then quietly pulled out of the garage, keeping the lights off, and drove down the street at a snail's pace.

22

The medical station was a few long metal trailers set up in rows in the middle of a Walmart parking lot. A few jeeps and Humvees were nearby, as were several groups of men in military uniforms.

Sam watched them closely. They were laughing and joking, and one of them had a cigarette dangling from his mouth. She watched the dim red glow as it rose and lowered. This was a conquering army celebrating its victory.

The guardsman got out with them and led them to the trailer at the center, the largest one. She didn't see a door anywhere, but another guard opened one from the inside to let them in.

Inside were several scientific workstations, complete with computers, microscopes, and MRI and CAT scan machines. Just behind the six employees at their stations was a clear glass wall that overlooked what appeared to be a surgical room with one hospital bed. The room was clean tile and shining chrome, and it looked untouched.

"Samantha?"

She turned to see Lt. General Clyde Olsen walk over to them. He was in full uniform and had grown a mustache that was speckled with gray. He smiled and put out his hand.

She shook it.

"What the hell are you doing here?"

"I could ask you the same thing."

He smirked. "I think you know. I read your CDC reports on the incident in Oahu."

"How did you get access to the CDC reports?"

"Come on, what do you think all this technology is for? Playing video games? Now what are you doing out here? I didn't authorize the CDC to come out."

"She's with me," Duncan said. "Dr. Duncan Adams, General. I'm with USAMRIID."

"Well, what exactly are *you* doing here?"

"Research, General."

"On what?"

"On the effects of Agent X on a civilian population. And the development of a possible vaccine."

"We have Agent X contained."

Duncan glanced at the surgical room. "It doesn't work that way. You can't contain something like this. It'll get out, and you'll need me to try and come up with a vaccine."

"Really?" He folded his arms. "You think you can come up with a vaccine?"

"I can try."

The lieutenant held Duncan's gaze a moment and then said, "Well, I guess we can use all the help we can get. Let me show you what we have."

He turned to one of the stations, and Sam and Duncan followed him. Numbers and a map of the state were up on the screen. Various swaths of the map were colored yellow, and red pinpoints marked other areas.

"Those red markers are known cases of viral infection," the general said. "We've got eighty-nine of them right now. All contained in quarantine. I sent several men to each location, and they're ensuring that the pathogen doesn't spread. The yellow is possible areas of infection, should one of the infected get out. Those are the areas where we've conducted our operation, containing the citizens so the infection can't spread. You can see that eighty of those eighty-nine are in southern California, so that's where we've focused."

"What about the rest of the state?" Sam asked.

"They're contained in their own way. All highways leading out of the state have been closed off, no planes or buses. Nothing. The only way someone can make it out of here is by sneaking through the desert, and we've got roving patrols and choppers for that."

Duncan shook his head. "Because that works so well on the Mexican border?"

The general didn't respond and instead pressed a button, bringing up an image of a young boy in a bed. The bedsheets and his hospital gown were stained black, and he appeared to have been burnt. But Sam had seen that condition enough to know that it wasn't a burn. The boy was hemorrhaging underneath his skin.

"Eighty-nine cameras feed into these trailers right here," he said. "We have someone watching all the infected, twenty-four, seven. As well as the men I have stationed there. No one in or out."

Sam stood silently for a long time as Duncan leaned close to the screen, observing the boy.

"This is monstrous," she said.

The general nodded. "It's... a trade-off. That's for sure. And no patchouli-smelling hippie was more against it than I was. But I have to follow orders."

"And what happens if someone tries to leave the state?" Duncan asked.

"They'll be arrested."

"Really?" Sam said. "A bunch of young soldiers are going to risk infection of the worst disease we've ever seen to stop a person from leaving? They're going to shoot them, Clyde."

"Only if they don't lie down and do what they're told. This is the American military, not the Visigoths."

"How did this happen?" Duncan finally asked.

"Someone from your little island in the Pacific got to the mainland. Three of them actually. Two of them died. One was alive for twenty-seven hours before she was..." He looked from one to the other. "Before she was eliminated. In those twenty-seven hours, she infected one other person, which led to this. Luckily, all of the original patients went immediately to the hospital as they'd heard about the symptoms, so we got them quarantined early."

She glanced at the boy on the screen. His eyes were halfway open as he slipped in and out of consciousness. "There is no way this agent was contained."

"Why not?"

"I saw it destroy Hawaii in less than three days. It's so contagious, just breathing the same air as an infected person could cause inhalation of the virus. I've never seen that. Not even with Ebola."

Olsen glanced at them both. "We've been developing something that could help us. It's almost ready for use, we think."

"What is it?" Duncan said.

"A vaccine."

23

Katherine Helmond sat in the driver's seat of her Audi at a red light and glanced at the other cars around her. One was full of twenty-something boys, who smiled at her and motioned for her to roll down the window. She turned and faced forward.

"Roll it down," Ian said.

"Why?"

"They've enough balls to flirt with someone with another man in the car. Let's see what they say."

"I don't want to."

Ian reached across her, leaning his arm against her chest, and his touch sent an icy chill down her spine as the window slowly withdrew into the door.

"Hey," one of the boys shouted, "why don't you come hop in with us?"

"Go ahead," Ian said.

"What d'ya mean?"

"Go get in with them."

She glanced at the men, and they were staring awkwardly at her, like adolescent boys who had never seen a girl before. "I don't understand."

"I'm telling you to get into the car with them. Go ahead. I won't stop you."

She glanced from him to the car and back.

"Better hurry before the light turns," he said.

She hesitated only a moment before opening the door and stepping out. The boy who had been speaking cheered, and his two friends were laughing. She glanced back at Ian, who was grinning calmly.

She ran over and jumped into the backseat. As the car pulled away, the boy in the passenger seat flipped Ian off and said, "What's up, nerd."

Katherine glanced back at her Audi. The car wasn't moving, and Ian was still sitting in the passenger seat. She turned forward, and the boy in the passenger turned around and said, "What's your name, sugar?"

"Don't slow down," she said. "Keep going."

"We're heading to a party down in West Hol'. You down?"

She scanned behind her. The Audi wasn't there.

Katherine saw only the headlights as they veered out of a side street, barreling toward the car she was in. She barely got out a scream before the Audi impacted against the sedan and sent it spinning into the intersection. Another car came from the other lane, blaring its horn as it tried to swerve, and clipped the sedan. The boy in the passenger seat flew out the window, his legs twisting unnaturally as his body squeezed through the small opening.

When the motion had stopped, her head hurt from hitting the roof. The boy next to her lay on top of her, unconscious, his head dribbling blood down over his face. She pushed him off, feeling pain in her wrists as she did so. The driver was groaning, and the flesh on the side of his head was exposed, spraying blood.

Her door opened and she stepped out, dizzy and with blood in her eyes. Someone grabbed her wrist, but she was too disoriented to scream. Only vague images filled her line of sight. Two people were shouting, and the spit from a silenced pistol followed, and then silence. She was forced into the driver's seat of an unfamiliar car, and someone sat next to her.

"You okay?" Ian asked.

"No."

"Let me drive."

She switched seats, still unsure where she was and what she was doing. Only motion and unclear pictures and colors were in her world, and she laid her head back and went to sleep.

When she woke, Katherine was in a hospital bed. The sheets were rough against her sensitive skin, and the lighting was too bright. She closed her eyes tightly, then rolled to the side and reopened them. A chubby nurse with blond hair was checking her IV.

"Where am I?"

The nurse smiled at her and came to the side of her bed. "You're in Good Samaritan. How are you feeling?"

"My head hurts."

She adjusted something and pressed a button. "That should help. Do you remember what happened?"

"I remember a car hitting us… not much else. Somebody in the seat next to me."

"It was probably your brother. He left for a bit but said he would be back."

"My brother?"

Images flooded her mind. She remembered a woman's neck breaking, someone shot to death at his door… and a man who laughed at all of it.

"You have to call the police," she said, panic rising in her voice. "I was kidnapped."

"Kidnapped by who, dear?"

"That man who said he was my brother. He kidnapped me. He was the one that caused the car wreck. Please, you have to call the police." She grabbed the nurse's hand. "Please. Please!"

"Okay, sweetheart. Okay, calm down. I'll call them, okay? You just sit tight. Okay? Can you do that for me?"

"Don't leave me alone," she said, nearly bursting into tears.

"Sweetheart, there's twenty people right outside this room. He's not going to do anything. We're going to take you down for your MRI in a minute anyway."

"Please don't leave."

"Okay, hold on. Hold on." The nurse lifted the pager strapped to her shoulder. "Amanda, you there?"

24

Howie drove so slowly, he wouldn't have been surprised if someone jogged past him. The streets were empty. The trucks and Humvees were using just the highways. But the choppers were always overhead, like vultures scavenging for a meal. Whenever lights flickered in the sky, he would pull to the curb and duck across the seats until the lights moved on.

Howie grew discouraged, knowing that Malibu was forty-two miles away and that the only way to get there was the Pacific Coast Highway. How was he going to dodge choppers on the PCH?

As he drove, he observed the empty houses, and a creeping feeling of melancholy and dread overtook him. It had taken so little to tear apart his entire world. The government had just decided to act, and he would never be the same. The most frightening part was imagining how far the government was going with this. Was the entire state shut down? Had they closed the whole country?

A chopper angled overhead, and he pulled into a driveway, parked, and turned off the car. The chopper banked left, sending the light down around him and flooding the car before disappearing over the tops of the trees. He didn't move for a long time. As he sat back up, he realized getting to Malibu like this was impossible. At this rate, he would need at least a day, and he certainly didn't want to be driving during daylight.

As he was debating what to do, something caught his attention—the outline of headlights. He ducked again, and a rattling engine rolled past him a bit, then stopped. He looked up over the door. A military jeep was parked in front of a house a few doors down. The brake lights were on, illuminating the darkness around the jeep with a bright red. They shut off, and a single uniformed man stepped out.

He glanced around slowly, all through the neighborhood. Then he turned to the house and went inside through the front door.

A few minutes later, he came out carrying a suitcase. He stuffed it in the back of the jeep and then went inside and came out maybe five minutes later with armfuls of electronics and silver.

When the man went back inside, Howie sat up. He saw himself in the rearview mirror and took a deep breath. He thought of Jessica and about the day she was born. The sound she made, her first sound, had never left him. He heard it in his dreams, and sometimes when he was newly divorced and living in an empty house, he swore he heard it in the house.

Nighttime was harder, and he remembered when she would run to him when he got home and say, "I missed you, Daddy." He couldn't remember the last time she'd called him Daddy.

He closed his eyes, then opened the door.

The night air was warm and still. For the first time he could remember, Los Angeles was quiet. The only noise was the sound of chopper blades, but they were far off.

Howie walked quickly to the front door and heard someone throwing drawers on the floor. He peeked inside and didn't see anything, so he took a few steps in. Another drawer crashed somewhere, and he followed the sound to where the man was standing in the kitchen, sifting through a cabinet that held various mementos and crystal.

Howie swallowed hard. The man's back was to him, and he was oblivious of everything around him. He assumed he was alone and didn't think twice about it. Howie glanced about... and spotted a rolling pin hanging on a hook. A golden thread strung through one end looped around the hook. He grabbed it and pulled it off.

Taking a deep breath, he stepped forward.

Only five feet or so separated him and the soldier. He was close enough to see the small hairs on the man's neck. He took another step, his foot coming down softly on the linoleum as he gently shifted his weight and brought his other leg in front of him. Sweat was dripping down his forehead into his eyes, but he didn't wipe it away.

The man was glaring at a silver bowl. He was about to toss it when he felt something and glanced back.

Their eyes met, but neither of them moved. They were like two men who shared a secret, and neither wanted to be the first to acknowledge that it existed.

The man's eyes went down to the rolling pin, and Howie's did, too. A grown man holding a rolling pin appeared so ridiculous, so cartoonish that he thought the soldier might burst out laughing. But he didn't. He stared at the rolling pin and then up to Howie.

The men stood there for what seemed like a long time, but was surely no more than a few seconds. The soldier reached for the pistol in a holster at his hip.

"No!" Howie shouted.

But it was too late. The pistol was coming out. Howie swung with all his strength and knocked the other man on the side of the head. He thought it would be like in the movies—a hard thump, like a baseball bat knocking against wood. Instead, the man's head was soft. And the blow was more like a fist hitting a melon, and he thought he could feel the side of the man's skull crack.

The soldier was down, twitching, and then he went limp. Howie dropped the rolling pin and kicked away the pistol that was in his hand. He bent down over the man and checked for a pulse. He still had one. Howie tried to wake him up but couldn't. The keys to the jeep were in his pocket, and Howie took them and held them tightly in his palm. He stood up, completely clueless as to what to do, when he heard another sound coming from outside—a jeep pulling to a stop.

He grabbed the pistol and ran around the house like a burglar trapped by a family coming home. He took the stairs to the second floor two at a time as he heard the voices of men entering the house. A brief silence was followed by shouting and the sound of boots stomping across linoleum.

Howie ran into a bedroom and to the window that looked down on a pool surrounded by a tall wooden fence. He ran back through the hallway and found another bedroom. This one looked out over the front lawn. He ran back to the window over the pool. As he opened it, he heard the men calling for additional troops and requesting a medic.

He crawled out on the sill and peered down. The drop was at least ten feet. He hung by his fingers to give him as much length as possible and then dropped. He hit the pool deck hard, sending a shock through his ankles. They stung, but he got up and ran toward the jeep as quickly as he could. The men were all inside the house, tearing it apart, looking for him. He jumped into the driver's seat and had to try three keys before he found the one that started the jeep.

Leaving as quietly as possible, he saw that one of the choppers had broken away from the rest and was headed his way.

25

Samantha was behind Dr. Olsen as he showed them an electron microscope prototype that he proudly told them had cost the military twenty-seven million dollars. It could enhance an image half the width of a hydrogen atom, making it the most powerful microscope in the world.

Samantha glanced inside. The image had a faint green tint. Bouncing around next to each other were what looked like bright-purple beanbag chairs. They contorted and then straightened again as they rubbed and bumped each other.

There were three ways to make a vaccine. The first was to weaken the pathogen. The virus, which would be too weak to reproduce, was then injected into the recipient's body. An immune response would still be generated, creating the antibodies that fought that virus for, typically, the rest of the recipient's life.

The second method was to destroy the virus and then insert the husk into the patient. Since the immune system had seen and could recognize the shell, the body would produce antibodies. The benefit was little risk of infection to the recipient.

And the third way was to remove one part of the virus and use that particular piece to elicit an immune response. This way worked well because the body only recognized a full, healthy virus, not just one part, and developed all the antibodies it would have during a full infection.

Sam thought that injecting a live or even weakened poxvirus into a recipient was too dangerous. If Olsen was smart, he would be using destroyed husks.

Sam had seen Agent X under an electron microscope, and she knew she was looking at an active virus, but it wasn't behaving normally. The virus was slow and seemed out of sync. Perhaps she was anthropomorphizing it, but she thought the virus was acting differently than it had the last time she'd seen it.

She deduced that Dr. Olsen must have chosen the first method of vaccine creation and had weakened the virus so that it could not reproduce.

"Have you done a phase three trial?" she asked, stepping away from the microscope.

"No," Olsen replied. "In fact, we haven't been able to do any substantial phase one studies. We've just never seen an organism like this. We maintain samples from the Oahu outbreak, but the ones found in the patients here are already different. In the span of a month, it's mutated."

Duncan had a look into the microscope. "I don't think this will work."

"Why not?" Olsen asked, seeming puzzled that he hadn't received a more positive reaction.

"The virus is too strong. It'll be able to replicate."

"We've monitored it after weakening, and it hasn't been able to. I think the chances are slim to none." He looked to Sam for confirmation. "What do you think?"

"I think Duncan's right. We don't fully understand what we're dealing with. Until more extensive studies can be performed, I wouldn't give anyone the vaccine."

He thought a moment and then said, "Dr. Bower, do you know why we dream?"

"No."

"An honest answer. I like that. There are over eleven hundred published theories as to why we dream, and that's all they are. Theories. Science cannot even answer the simple question of why we dream, something Cro-Magnon man quite possibly asked himself, and we've been unable to answer since. So if, with all our knowledge, we cannot even say why we dream, how are we supposed to know for certain what an organism one billionth our size will do? We just have to take our chances."

Sam nodded toward the microscope. "Viruses aren't like other organisms, Clyde. They're as old as life itself and have lived through every cataclysm that has wiped out most other species. They adapt, they hide when threatened, and some people believe they can even feel pain. And this one we have is the deadliest I've ever seen. How can you even think about injecting it into people? Weakened or not?"

"Because that's all I have." He checked his watch. "The first batch of volunteers should be here shortly to accept the vaccine. I could really use a good pair of extra hands to administer it."

"I'll help." She paused. "There is one other thing. My sister was here, and I've lost contact with her."

His brow furrowed. "I'm sorry. If she's in one of our camps, she'll have to stay there for the time being. There're plenty of guards and food, and she won't be mistreated. But I can't get her out right now."

"You can't, or you won't?"

"I suppose if you want to put it that way, then I won't."

"Why is this even necessary? Just have quarantine zones for the infected. You don't need to put everybody in prison."

"That's the order from on high, so that's what I'm going to do. Sorry, Sam. You know I want to help you. But she has to stay where she is."

"Can you at least tell me where she is so I can check on her and see if she needs anything?"

He thought a moment. "Okay, I'll find out. Just give me her name and birthday."

26

In the middle of the night, Samantha stretched and decided she needed some caffeine if she was going to stay up, giving doses of the vaccine. Since the vaccine hadn't gone through the proper clinical studies, she was uncomfortable injecting it into human subjects. But she'd thought about it on the drive out of the medical center to downtown and couldn't think of another option. If the vaccine worked, it would prevent an enormous amount of suffering. But if it didn't, if Duncan was right and the virus was strong enough to replicate in a weakened state, everyone vaccinated would be infected.

She sat in the passenger seat this time, and Duncan was in the backseat. She glanced over at him, and his head was leaned against the seat. He was sleeping, even though the jeep bounced around as if they were on an unpaved African road rather than a highway in Los Angeles.

Duncan was a decent man, and she knew he cared for her deeply. They had some points of contention, particularly religion. She saw it as an unnecessary extravagance. Why put in all that time and effort worshiping ghosts that likely didn't exist? Atheism was as illogical to her because it was a belief system built around a negative of something that was non-verifiable. She had gone to a meeting at a local atheist organization, but she'd found it just as formulaic as the religious services she'd been to.

Duncan, with both a medical degree and a PhD in microbiology, was quite likely the most brilliant man she had ever known. She was puzzled that this brilliant man could believe in things without evidence and apply the scientific method all day at work, then abandon it when it came to his own fundamental beliefs.

Her father had been the same. He'd been a devout Catholic his entire life and read *History of the Saints* and the New Testament to her as bedtime stories when she was three years old. She particularly enjoyed *History of the Saints*, the stories of men and women of conviction who were ready to die in the most gruesome ways for their faith. She could think of few things—in fact nothing—that inspired as much passion as faith. The whole thing was an enigma to her. Religious thinking seemed to be declining in the Western world, with only five percent of Europeans attending church and the number of regular attendees declining in the United States. Societies had been religious for so long—for the entire existence of mankind, in fact—that she couldn't decide how the complete abandonment of religion would impact society. She could think of only two possibilities: enlightenment or anarchy.

"It's right up here, Dr. Bower," the driver said.

The jeep came to a stop, and she stepped out as the rough halt roused Duncan. A metal trailer, much like the one Dr. Olsen had occupied with his equipment and surgical room, was set up for them. As they stepped inside, the driver got out boxes of pre-wrapped syringes filled with the vaccine. He placed them down near some chairs and glanced at both of them. "Good luck."

When they were alone, Duncan sat down. He seemed tired and uncertain of what they should be doing.

"I don't think this is going to work," he said.

"I know."

"So if it doesn't, we're injecting these people with replicating poxvirus."

"I know," she said softly.

He exhaled. "What a mess. I can't believe it's come to this. We have to potentially kill several hundred people to see if we can save several billion." He leaned back in the chair. "I read an account once from a historian that was alive during the Plague of Justinian in Constantinople. He said the levies holding back flooding waters broke because the people that maintained them had grown sick. And when they broke, the city was flooded. Sitting by his window, he watched the bodies float down his street. He said the city was choked with corpses to the point that people felt like they couldn't breathe…"

"And it faded away, Duncan. At some point, this will fade away, too."

"In the meantime, before the plague faded away, it changed the course of history and killed five thousand people a day. And this pathogen is more contagious. I'm no big-government nut, by any means, but I'm not sure I'm against all this." He waved his hand around the trailer. "We're not talking a few thousand or even a hundred thousand deaths, Sam. We're talking about the end of civilization."

"And so because of that risk, we throw out our values, our beliefs? We toss them to try and have a little more safety? It's not worth it. I'd rather die out than live in Stalinist Russia. That type of life isn't life at all."

He rubbed his temples. "Maybe any life is better than no life."

Before she could respond, a middle-aged blond woman in a purple shirt appeared at the door.

"I was brought here for the vaccine," she said. "I was told to get it here."

Sam glanced at Duncan, then told the woman, "Come in and roll up your sleeve, please."

27

Ian waited around the corner after ramming the Audi into the car full of boys. No police or ambulances arrived since no one's cell phone worked. He took out his own, connected to a private server, and connected directly with the hospital. After giving them the address, he walked away with a limp because his knee had butted into the dash.

The building he had come for wasn't more than a mile away. He watched the cars pass him as he limped down the sidewalk, until he came across a pharmacy. Inside, the pharmacist and a tech were behind the counter, trying to get their Internet connections to work.

Ian went to an empty aisle and pulled down his pin-striped trousers. His injured knee wasn't bleeding at all, which signified an internal injury. It felt a bit as if he'd torn his ACL or MCL. But he didn't have time for that. He grabbed two ACE bandages and wrapped them tightly around the knee.

He left the store and headed farther down the street, to the building he was searching for. He didn't have to double-check the list. He had memorized every name and address.

The building was almost a skyscraper, with maybe fifteen or sixteen stories. On the tenth floor was a man named Gabriel Vega, a Mexican national who worked for the United Nations and was only in Los Angeles for a brief meeting with officials from the consulate.

Ian hobbled inside. Flowers decorated the dark-wood-paneled lobby, and the elevators were chrome. An older security guard sitting next to them looked up.

"Can I help y—"

Two slugs entered his left eye, the second following the first almost perfectly, breaking through the back of his skull with a dull thump as he toppled over his chair. The elevator dinged, and Ian stepped on and glanced up at the mirrored ceiling as it began to rise.

How many elevators like this have I been in? he wondered. How many people above him were living their lives in total obliviousness while death quietly drifted up to them? That their decisions had led to a visit from him was an odd thought to consider. From the moment they were born, they were making choices, and their choices brought him to them. The truly interesting question was whether someone was riding an elevator up for him.

The doors opened on the tenth floor, where he got out. Elegant lights were spaced in the hallway, and the carpet was a pure white, without a trace of dirt. And a unique thing for this city, it had no smell—no exhaust, no perfume, no warm garbage, or sweat. The place was odorless and lifeless.

He found the apartment he wanted and knocked. Footsteps came from inside, then the door opened. An elderly Hispanic man, perhaps as old as eighty or eighty-five, answered the door.

"I'm looking for Gabriel," Ian said.

"Who are you?" the man replied in heavily accented English.

"A friend. My name's Ian."

He was silent a moment. "You're a friend of my grandson's?"

"Yes."

"Gabriel, *venir aqui*."

"*Que?*" A young man of twenty-six or twenty-seven came to the door.

Ian eyed him up and down. "Are you Gabriel?"

"Yeah."

"You work at the consulate? On cross-border epidemiological issues?"

He gave his grandfather a quizzical glance and said, "Yes."

Ian lifted the pistol and fired into the boy's chest. It threw him back against the wall, leaving a smear of blood all the way down as he slid to the floor. The grandfather's eyes went wide, but he didn't have time for much more of a reaction. Ian slammed his elbow into the old man's throat, crushing the windpipe, and then swept his feet out from under him. The old man fell so hard, Ian heard his delicate bones crack as they broke. He stepped over him, leaving the grandfather gasping for breath on his back like an injured turtle, and shut the door behind him.

Ian fired one more round into the boy's heart to be sure he was dead and went farther in to the apartment. One bedroom was a master decorated with furniture that was at least thirty years too old. The other was decorated with baseball caps and sports memorabilia. Ian walked into this one and glanced around.

Photos were up on the nightstand of the boy and his grandfather at baseball games and on a fishing trip. He saw all of Gabriel's life then. His parents had abandoned him at a young age, and a kindly grandfather who had thought he'd already put in his time raising his children had taken him in and raised him as his own.

Ian did not like remorse or guilt. They were wasted emotions the herd felt because they had been trained from childhood to have a response to stimuli that shouldn't have meant anything. Emotions were nothing more than a response of the weak, those who were ruled over rather than doing the ruling. Successful people were frequently on television, discussing love, charity, and compassion, but those were not the things that had made them successful. They shared a secret that they would never reveal. The formula for success was simple enough for anyone that wanted to learn it: do not feel guilt.

Still, in his own way, Ian was saddened that the grandfather had to die and that he had seen his grandson die before him. If he had it to do again, Ian would kill the grandfather first.

Ian checked the rest of the apartment, and no one was there. He made his way down the elevator, and when he stepped off, a crowd had gathered around the security guard's body. They were all trying cell phones, sending texts to nowhere, and placing calls that would never connect. They seemed so impotent that Ian almost laughed. He brushed past them, getting a good look at their faces. Absolutely fascinating, they were much like a different species he couldn't possibly empathize with. They fussed over this man whom they had never met. They probably saw him every day and ignored him, but once he was dead, they cared for him. *What a waste of energy.*

Three names were left on his list. He thought about commandeering a car, but something about Katherine was… entertaining. He couldn't put his finger on why, but he enjoyed her company.

He hailed a cab to take him to the hospital.

28

Samantha held the syringe above the pale dermis of the woman's bicep. Wearing thin latex gloves and a surgical mask, Samantha glanced once at Duncan, then plunged the needle into the doughy flesh. She injected the weakened pathogen. Agent X, the deadliest aspect of nature she had ever encountered, was flowing in this woman's veins. And they would have to hope that it didn't kill her.

The situation was so absurd that she questioned if they should be there at all. But as Duncan had pointed out, the risk of death was worth the reward of a cure. Maybe he was right, but they were still dealing with one unknown by instituting another.

She pulled out the syringe, threw it into a biohazard bin sitting next to them, and leaned back in the chair as Duncan slapped a cotton ball and a Band-Aid on the woman's arm.

"So is that all? Can I go home now?"

"I don't know," Samantha said. "Where are you staying?"

"They got these, well, I don't know what you'd call them. Communes, I guess. They got these communes set up, and they have cots for us. And we're just supposed to sleep out there. But I wanna go home. I need my medications, and they said they was gonna go get 'em, but they never did."

Duncan rose. "We'll let you know."

He led her outside, where a line of at least a hundred people had formed.

Getting through everyone took several hours because more truckloads of people showed up. They had been told, Samantha was informed, that if they submitted to the shot, they could go home in two days.

Samantha was cleaning the site of the injection with alcohol for a teenage girl, who asked, "So where did the sickness come from?"

"The sickness?" Samantha asked.

"That's what they call it. The sickness. Where'd it come from?"

"Well," she said, preparing the syringe, "sometimes nature just throws viruses at us. They pop up, do a lot of damage, and then disappear." She thrust the needle into the girl's arm. "There was a flu in 1918 that killed almost a million people and then just disappeared. It came and went. And sometimes these things are released accidentally by people that are studying them. And other times, we have no idea where they come from."

"That's scary."

"Yeah," she said, taking off her surgical mask. "It is. You're done. Leave the Band-Aid on at least an hour."

"Thanks."

When the girl had left, Sam stepped outside into the night air and stretched her back. She glanced up to the moon as Duncan came out and sat on one of the steps of the trailer. He leaned back on his elbows. "Where you staying tonight?"

"I didn't even think about it. I was hoping at Jane's in-laws' house."

"We can probably get a ride down there, unless they've already been rounded up."

Sam pulled out her cell phone and saw she had a voice mail. She turned the sound on and listened to it.

"Sam, Clyde Olsen. Your sister is being held at one of our facilities. If you want to visit her, you can. I've given you clearance. She's at facility One-Nine-Two-Two. It's in Rustic Canyon. Give me a text when you're done with the vaccinations, and I'll send a jeep up to drive you."

She hung up and texted back the number, stating that they were done and needed a ride. She got a text back. *Okay.* Nothing else.

"What is it?" Duncan asked.

"My sister's being held at one of their facilities."

"Are they going to let you see her?"

"Yeah, Clyde said he's cleared me."

He got up and stretched his arms over his head. "Sam, are you sure you want to see her locked in a cage?"

"What else am I supposed to do? Bury my head in the sand?"

"She's going to be fine. This… thing just needs to get sorted out."

"Sorted out by who, Duncan? How many people know what's going on here?"

"I don't know."

She tapped the cell phone against her chin. "I need to figure out a way to get her out of this state. Is there anything you can do?"

"I can take one person on a flight with me, not two. And especially not a family with kids."

She started to say something, but her voice was drowned out by the sound of helicopter blades hovering above them.

29

The air was warm and tasted like salt so close to the ocean. The palm trees on the side of the interstate were swaying lightly with the breeze, but Howie Burke couldn't enjoy the view because of the noise—rumbling diesel engines and choppers thumping in the air.

The jeep he was driving had a top, but no doors. He had searched it and found no uniforms, so he never rode along with other trucks or jeeps. He always stayed behind, hoping they wouldn't bother checking to see who was driving.

Though the interstate had a fair amount of military traffic, it was nothing compared to the usual everyday traffic of any highway in Los Angeles, and he was making extraordinary time. And it didn't hurt that no traffic cops or Highway Patrol officers were anywhere in sight. Within twenty minutes, he was in Malibu.

He stopped somewhere near the beach, close enough that he saw the twirling barbed wire on the top of the cage. They had added more cots and fences, but they were guarded by fewer troops, towers, and military vehicles. They were stretched thin and clearly hadn't planned for the influx of people.

No one was on the street, and Howie turned the jeep off and got out. He was perhaps a block from the entrance to the cage. Walking through the night air in a dead silence was one of the most chilling experiences he had ever had. Something about a forced quiet over an entire section of the biggest city in the world was unnerving—not something he had ever thought he would experience.

As he drew near, he saw the layout well. Of the three towers in the immediate vicinity, only one was guarded, and the soldier was leaning back with his rifle sitting next to him. He was staring blankly over the city and would glance down occasionally at the people lying on the cots, covered with gray blankets even though it was probably eighty degrees.

Howie waited behind a cluster of palm trees. He wasn't sure exactly what he was going to do. Even though there were only about five guards anywhere near the fence, that was five too many. He was no fighter or soldier.

He tried to spot Jessica through the fence, but the floodlights had been dimmed, and all he saw were indistinct bumps lying on cots.

Howie thought briefly about ramming the jeep through the fence, but the guards might open fire and hit Jessica. Staring at the two entrances again, he was wondering if he could get into the back one when he heard something behind him.

Turning around, he saw a man in a military uniform holding a rifle. He was playing on his phone and not paying attention; he hadn't seen him.

Howie moved first. He jumped on the guard, taking him down to the ground. They were both around the same weight with similar builds, and neither of them could get an advantage. Howie had his hands wrapped around the rifle, and the man was grunting as he tried to push him off.

Just don't yell, Howie thought. *Please don't yell.*

The guardsman twisted the rifle around, and it smacked Howie in the eye, slamming that eye closed. He tried to swing again, and Howie lurched back. The rifle missed his face by only inches. Howie then got on top of the rifle, his hands spread evenly on it, and pushed his bodyweight down. The rifle pressed against the guardsman's throat, strangling him.

The guardsman tried yelling, but the rifle was pressed so hard into his windpipe that just a squeak came out of him. He was pushing against the rifle, but didn't have good leverage, and soon, his hands weren't a factor. Howie was pressing with everything he had, his shoulders straining, veins sticking out in his forearms.

The guardsman tried kicking up with his legs to get enough momentum to throw Howie off, but he couldn't do it. He tried one last time to twist the rifle away from his throat. Instead, it got a better angle on the windpipe. Within a few moments, he'd passed out.

Howie lifted the rifle in the air, aiming the butt at the man's head. He could crush it with enough blows, and the man wouldn't even feel any pain. Howie pictured himself doing that. But it didn't happen. As alien as this situation was, he couldn't do something so out of character.

Moving quickly, he took the guardsman's uniform and dumped his own clothes in the bushes. The uniform was slightly smaller and was tucked too snugly in the crotch. The name sewn into the uniform over the chest said Sanders. Howie took the rifle and jogged over to the entrance of the cage.

30

The helicopter, a dull green with gray splotches, touched down not far from where Samantha was standing. She watched as two men came out, ducking their heads low, though they couldn't possibly have touched the rotating blades unless they jumped. One of them was Clyde Olsen.

"Tell me you didn't go through that entire batch of vaccines?" he said, coming up to them.

"Isn't that the point?" Duncan asked.

His face contorted as if he'd eaten something sour. "The vaccines were… ineffective. We had inoculated a group about five hours before you'd arrived… They're beginning to show symptoms."

"Symptoms?" Sam said angrily.

"It was a risk we had to take, and they were fully informed. They chose to take it."

"They shouldn't be displaying symptoms for at least a day," Duncan said.

"It's… The damn thing is mutating so fast, we can't keep up. Its incubation period has gone from seventy-two hours down to four."

"We have to get these people quarantined," Sam said.

"Already taken care of. I… uh, about the vaccines… One of the groups… I don't quite know how to say this."

Samantha's stomach was in knots. He didn't have to say it. She already knew. Her sister had been one of the ones inoculated.

The jeep came not long after Olsen had left. He'd asked that they come with him in the chopper, but Sam had refused, and Duncan stayed with her. She was going to visit her sister, no matter what—even through a plastic barrier.

When the jeep arrived, the driver was a young woman in a beige uniform. Samantha and Duncan climbed in, and she spun it around, then headed through Los Angeles.

"Sorry I was late," she said. "We were quarantining a new part of the city, and I had to help. It's chaos that first hour."

The driver took the interstate and then the back roads. The route took them away from downtown and farther up into the hills, near hiking and biking trails. Trees surrounded them, and the air was cool and crisp. Worry gnawed at Samantha's guts as Duncan was slowly dozing off. His eyes would shut and then dart open. Sam saw him pinching himself to try to stay awake, sticking his head out the window to let the wind hit him, and shifting positions, but nothing seemed to work.

Soon, Samantha saw what they had come for, and it terrified her.

The fence was about twelve feet high and tipped with looping barbed wire with makeshift towers around the perimeter. At the entrance sat a guard at a desk. Inside were hundreds and hundreds of cots with gray blankets. Men and women were separated by a partition but could still see and talk to one another through it.

As far as she could tell, it was a concentration camp.

"How did you decide who to bring here?" Sam asked.

The woman replied, "They started with certain parts of the city, like Beverly Hills and Malibu, and then we're kind of getting the rest of the city. We should have everywhere in like a day or something."

She hopped out of the jeep, but Duncan and Sam didn't move.

He said, "I'm sorry, Sam."

Sam didn't respond. The only thought in her mind was that her sister was in that place, tucked away like some rat waiting to be experimented on in a university laboratory. And on top of that, she had just injected live viruses into over a hundred people. The staggering repercussions made her feel nauseated. But she couldn't think about that. She had to focus on her sister; she could wallow in guilt later.

She got out of the jeep and followed the woman, who led her to the entrance. All the guards were wearing surgical masks.

The one at the entrance turned to the woman. "Who's this?"

"They need to see one of the quarantined. What was her name?"

"Jane Bower is her maiden name, but she'd likely be under Jane Gates."

The man scanned a list on an iPad. "Okay, she's here. I got a note that says her sister's coming to visit her. I guess that's you."

He stood up and unlocked a gate on the women's side. He pressed a button on the PA system. "Jane Bower or Jane Gates to the front entrance."

They waited a few moments, and no one came forward. He repeated into the device, "Jane Bower or Jane Gates to the front entrance now."

Another few minutes passed, and still, nothing.

"She ain't here," the guardsman said.

"General Olsen told me she was."

The guardsman scanned the iPad again. "Oh, here she is. She's on my list of people that have been shipped out."

"Shipped out where?"

"Quarantine."

"You have people in cages, and you don't think that's quarantine?"

"I mean like real quarantine. With no one else around them."

"Where is that?"

"I can't tell you. It's classified."

"General Olsen gave me specific permission to see my sister, and I want to see her now."

"Well, that's fine, but I ain't gonna be the one to tell you where she is. Go ask General Olsen."

31

Kyle Levitt had joined the National Guard when he was eighteen years old. The recruiter at his school had been a cool guy named Dave. He drove a Viper and would show up to the school with his sleeves rolled up, revealing muscular arms, and Kyle saw the way the girls stared at him.

Kyle had planned on becoming a veterinarian, but one meeting with Dave had changed his mind.

"Vets don't get no pussy," Dave had told him.

Instead of discussing it with his parents, Kyle had prayed about it and decided that the Lord wanted him to join the National Guard. He had even had a dream telling him something like that. He thought, as Dave had promised, he would be fighting for God and country against Bin Laden. But when he was shipped off to Iraq for his first tour in 2006, he didn't see Bin Laden. He saw peasants fighting not only the terrorists, but the coalition soldiers, as well.

He'd had several close calls in Iraq. One stuck more than the others; an IED had gone off about four feet from the vehicle he was riding in. The Humvee in front of them was blown to hell, and so much shrapnel flew off that some of it burst through their windshield and hit him in the face. Luckily, he hadn't taken any permanent damage other than a scar on his cheek.

As Kyle walked the perimeter of the huge fence, what the guardsmen had named the Cage, he felt as though he were back in Iraq, on patrol, ensuring the enemy combatants weren't attempting to escape from custody.

But he wasn't in Iraq. He was twenty-five miles from where he had grown up in Santa Monica. And the people inside the cage weren't enemy combatants; they were Americans.

Some of the other soldiers fell into their roles perfectly and treated the Americans no differently from the Iraqis they had dealt with. As far as they were concerned, they followed orders, and nothing else mattered. But for Kyle, it was more complicated. He felt for these people, and his entire family was in this city. Would they be rounded up, too? Would he be expected to guard his own family with a rifle pointed at their heads?

Fuck that, he thought. He would go AWOL first and take his family with him.

But something more concerning was beginning to happen. He'd been coughing for about a day, and the night before, he'd had a fever and diarrhea. He was still hot and couldn't stop sweating. He had dumped ice water over his head, but that didn't feel like it did anything. A few minutes later, he would be burning up again.

His stomach convulsed, and he felt his bowels let loose. He ran to a row of nearby bushes and vomited. The vomit was clear and black, but something like dark oatmeal came up with it. The fluid spattered over the bushes and didn't seem to stop until it decided it was done.

The vomiting alleviated the pain in his guts for a few minutes, and then the tight, aching pain returned and he had to vomit again.

He walked to the front entrance, where his buddy Mark was stationed.

"You all right, man?" Mark asked.

"No. I gotta go."

"Where?"

"Barracks, man. I'm not feelin' hot. Flu or somethin'."

Mark glanced around to make sure no one else was listening. "That ain't no damn flu, you fucking idiot. Tell me you didn't take off your mask when you was dealin' with these folks."

He shook his head. "No. I don't think so… I can't remember."

Mark peered at a group of other soldiers near a tower. "Get outta here, now. I'll cover for you. Just take a jeep and go, and don't come back until you feel better. And you ain't goin' near the barracks, you hear me? You go straight to the med tent."

"Thanks."

He found a jeep with the keys in the ignition. He wasn't supposed to commandeer a vehicle without permission, but Mark, who was his superior, had just given him what sounded like permission. Even though Mark probably didn't rank high enough to give permission like that, it didn't matter. Kyle could barely stand.

He drove off the camp and took the side streets rather than the 405 or the PCH. The streets were empty, and it felt eerie, like the zombie apocalypse he was always afraid of as a child.

He drove for at least half an hour and kept feeling worse. In that short span of time, he'd had to stop three times to vomit, and he had grown certain, considering that he hadn't eaten or drank anything for four hours, that he was vomiting pure blood.

Driving into Burbank, a part of the city that wasn't quarantined yet, he found a hotel on one of the streets leading to downtown. He parked in front and didn't move for a long time, closing his eyes and tilting his face up to the sky. He turned the jeep back on and pulled away. His mind was hazy, and he wasn't sure where he was going or what he was doing.

The streets weren't empty there, and he had a hard time keeping up with traffic. His vision was getting blurry, and the constant vomiting had burst the blood vessels in his eyes. He could see the red strands running along the whites of his eyes in the rearview mirror. He felt it as a sharp pain in his head and eyes.

At a stoplight, he stumbled out of the jeep and over to the car next to him. The driver was a portly man with glasses, and his wife was in the passenger seat with the window down.

"Excuse me," Kyle said, slurring his speech. "Where is the hospit—"

Vomit spurted out of his mouth and over the woman. It hit her in the face and dripped down onto her white blouse and her neck, making her look like a murder victim. Kyle's head spun, and he tumbled backward.

He heard her screaming and the frantic voice of the husband trying to calm her down.

32

Katherine sat up in the hospital bed and pressed the call button for the nurse. The nurse took almost five minutes to get back.

"What do you need, dear?"

"Did you call the police?"

The nurse took a few steps around the room, checking the equipment. "None of the phones are working. We're having some sort of blackout or something, dear. I don't even know how they found out about you, because none of our phones have been working for a while."

"So you don't have any police here?"

"'Fraid not. But relax. You can stay here until we figure something out."

The nurse checked her IV, which was empty, and then removed the bag and replaced it with a new saline solution before pressing a few buttons on a machine and leaving the room. Katherine leaned her head back on the pillow and stared at the ceiling. She wondered where her dad was and imagined the panic that must have gripped him when she hadn't shown up at the airport or answered her phone.

Suddenly, she became aware that someone had walked into her room though she hadn't heard anything. Ian was standing at the doorway. He grinned and sat down in the chair next to the bed.

Unable to say anything, she sobbed.

"You didn't miss me?" he asked.

"Please just kill me," she cried, covering her face with her hands.

"I don't want to kill you."

"Why are you doing this? Who are these people? What have they done that they have to die?"

Ian put his foot on the bed and pushed himself back, balancing on two legs of the chair. "It's not what they've done. It's what they're likely to do. They are trying to stop something that my employers don't want stopped. They'll become leaders in a movement to stop it. An army of sheep led by a lion is more powerful than an army of lions led by a sheep."

She wiped at the tears, shaking her head. "I don't understand."

"The world's changing, Katherine. A new one is on the way. And certain people aren't welcoming of the new."

"Please leave me alone, please."

"I promise that I won't harm you."

"I'm at the hospital. You've already harmed me."

He was silent.

"They told me one of the boys is in critical condition. Why did you do that? Why would you hurt people if you don't have to?"

Ian grew visibly uncomfortable and then licked his lips. Katherine noticed that a small strand of drool was coming off his lower lip, and he suctioned it up with his tongue.

"Who knows why we do what we do? Are you well enough to walk on your own, or should I get a wheelchair?"

"Why me? Why did you choose me?"

He rose. "Let's go."

A red Audi of the same model as her car was out front. Ian held open the door for her, and she got inside. He went to the driver's side, got in, and pulled away from the hospital.

He wiped his mouth again, making sure no more drool was leaking out of him—a side effect of the medication he had been taking, as was occasionally slurred speech. He would have to watch himself more closely.

"It's your car now," he said. "One year newer."

"I don't want it."

"Why not?"

"Because I don't want something that you killed to get."

"Who said anything about killed? I bought this for you. Look at the licensing on the back window. It was purchased today. Cost me forty grand. Plus an extra five to get the dealer to come in at this hour."

She glanced back and saw the yellow tag with the date. "Why would you buy me a car?"

"Because I ruined your last one. It's only fair."

She shook her head, staring out the window at the passing homes and trees that swayed in the darkness like shadows. "I don't understand this. I don't know why I'm here."

"There's only three more names on the list. After that, I'll let you go. I promise."

"Who are the three people?"

"No one you'd know. The next one is a man that works for the National Security Administration. He's thinking about leaking information about the imprisonments."

"What imprisonments?"

"Oh, that's right," he said with a grin. "You don't know. They're rounding everyone up. Anyone displaying symptoms of a certain disease is taken to various hospitals for personal quarantine. Everyone else not displaying symptoms are taken to cages set up in fields and on beaches, in the middle of streets…"

Her stomach dropped. "What about my dad?"

"What about him?"

"Where is he?"

"I don't know. If he had arrived in LA before they shut flights down, he'd be in a cage. But I'm guessing he never made it out here."

For a long time, she was quiet, staring out the window. In college, the school had had an earthquake scare once, and everyone had panicked and run out of the building. Going outside was the last thing you were supposed to do, and everyone had known better, but they'd done it anyway.

Under stress, people's reasoning broke. Their calm broke. They did what their reptilian brains told them to do. She had known this her entire life. But something was different about the man sitting next to her. He wasn't like that. Even when he was murdering people, he was completely calm, without a trace of emotion.

His eyes were forward, concentrating on the road. She was embarrassed of the thought, but it crossed her mind that he was extraordinarily good looking. She wondered why someone with his talent, intelligence, and looks would choose to do what he did. Murderers were supposed to be the monsters that hid under our beds, not someone who could be in a J. Crew catalogue.

"What's really going on?" she asked softly.

He glanced at her and then back out at the road. "You wouldn't believe me if I told you."

33

Howie stopped about a dozen feet from the entrance to the cage. He swallowed hard, not so much from nervousness but because of an itch he'd been having in his throat. He was still sweating although he didn't feel like he should be, and a general malaise was coming over him. He ignored it, attributing it to fatigue, and went forward.

The guard at the entrance looked up. Howie didn't recognize him.

"Hey, how are ya?" Howie said.

"Good."

"Here for two people. They're being transferred up to the Hills."

The man pulled out his iPad and opened a document. "What two people?"

"Jessica Burke and Harold Burke."

He flipped through the document for a moment. "Okay, where they going again?"

"Facility up in the Hills. I don't know why. Lieutenant just said to come get 'em and take 'em up."

"Lieutenant Edmonds?"

"Yeah."

The man thought for a moment. "I'm gonna call and verify really quick."

Howie swallowed and felt the sweat slowly trickle off his head and down his neck. "Listen, I was supposed to take these two up there at the beginning of the night and screwed up. You call the lieutenant, and he's gonna chew my ass, brother."

The man thought for a few seconds and said, "Fine. Just get 'em outta here quick."

The guard let Howie into the cage. He walked toward the back. On a cot with her legs crossed, her head tilted to the side, was Jessica, fast asleep. In the cot next to hers was Mike. His cot was pulled closer and to the front of Jessica's. Howie knelt beside her and glanced at the guard at the entrance. He wasn't paying attention.

"Jessica," he whispered.

Her eyes opened, and he put a finger to his lips, indicating for her to be quiet. She sat up and put her arms around his neck. He didn't know how to respond at first, and then he hugged her back—something he hadn't done since she was a child.

He said, "Let's go."

Mike had woken. "How'd you get back here?"

"I'll tell you later. Come on, I got you outta here, too."

"How?"

"Don't worry about how. If anyone asks, your name is Harold Burke. Let's go before they change their mind."

They walked in front as Howie stayed behind them. He nodded to the guard at the entrance, who was eyeing him. The guard watched them a good five or six seconds before returning to what he was doing.

161

As soon as they got around the corner and out of sight of the guard, Howie said, "Run, now."

The metal of the jeep groaned as all three jumped in. Howie turned the ignition and spun a U-turn, then headed down the block before turning onto Belvedere, toward the city.

34

Samantha sat in the passenger seat of the military jeep parked in front of Los Angeles County General Hospital. The building was white with neon-green trim. The parking lot was nearly empty. They got out of the jeep, and the driver informed them she would wait there.

Clyde Olsen had told them where to find Jane. He was reluctant to hand over the information once he'd heard that she'd been put into personal quarantine. "Sam, I don't think this is going to end well for her," he'd said.

But Samantha had insisted that she needed to see her sister.

Jane Bower Gates was a classically trained violinist who played for the Seattle Symphony Orchestra. While Sam had always been assertive and daring, Jane was softer and more sensitive. She lived in her own world, and music had always been her escape. After initially wanting to go into a career in mathematics, Jane had changed majors as an undergraduate at the last moment in her senior year and completed three years' worth of music courses in three semesters.

There had always been a little bit of a rivalry between them when they were younger, each trying to prove to their parents she was smarter than the other. At the time, the competition was annoying and stressful, but as Samantha grew older, she understood that most families emphasized looks, not intellect. And she was grateful that it hadn't been that way in their home.

On the day Jane got married, she told Samantha that she had been her role model and that she'd switched from mathematics to music because she saw how passionately Sam pursued medicine. Samantha had forgotten that she'd told her sister to do what she loved and that if she loved doing something, she would eventually make money at it, regardless of the short-term consequences. Jane told her that that had changed her life.

"You sure you want to see this?" Duncan asked.

Samantha started to say something, but no words came. Her eyes welled up with tears against her will, and she put her hand to her mouth as the tears rolled down her cheeks. Duncan put his arms around her, and they stood silently in the night for a moment before going inside.

The hospital was like any other: harsh lighting, the smell of antiseptic and stale air conditioning, and linoleum floors that needed mopping. The reception desk was staffed by two young women, and Samantha went to them and asked for the quarantine floor.

"Um, you can't go up there," one of the receptionists said.

Duncan pulled out a military badge. "We're fine."

The girl was young and probably had never been in a situation like this before. She stared pleadingly at the other girl, who shrugged.

"Um, well, okay. I guess."

They took the elevator to the psychiatric wing and got off on the third floor. They followed the signs on the walls to where two soldiers stood by the door. These weren't national guardsmen, though. These guys wore Rangers' uniforms, and Sam wondered why they would be watching the quarantined patients.

Duncan showed them his badge.

"Sorry, sir," one said. "We can't let anyone through."

"Her sister is in there. She wants to see her, and was given permission. And that comes directly from General Olsen. Call him if you have an issue, but I don't think he's going to like getting woken up in the middle of the night for something he's already given permission for."

The Ranger had the same look as the receptionist's, though he was much more decisive. "One moment." The Ranger took out a cell phone and spoke quietly for a few seconds. She couldn't hear what he was saying, but Sam made out the last two words. "Sorry, sir."

"Go in. You can't go behind the plastic barrier. If you do, our orders are to quarantine you, as well."

"We won't. Thank you."

Samantha opened the door. Jane was lying back in bed, with her eyes closed. Her hair was onyx black, and her face had perfect proportions. Samantha had always thought Jane was the prettier sister, though Jane thought the same thing of her.

A thick plastic canopy over her bed was taped to the floor to keep anything from coming in or out. A small air pump connected to the power socket inside the canopy recycled the stale air, and a plastic tube that vented the carbon dioxide stuck out from the top.

Samantha took one of the two chairs against the wall and brought it near the canopy. She watched her sister's chest go up and down. Slowly, Jane's eyes opened. They expressed surprise at first, and then she smiled. The smile was so weak, and her lips so dry and cracked from dehydration, that Samantha nearly burst into tears again.

"Hey," Jane said softly.

"I missed you, Janey. How are you feeling?"

"Like I ate a hot dog from a gas station at three in the morning."

Samantha, though maintaining eye contact as much as possible, was evaluating her. Jane had no hemorrhaging underneath her skin, and other than the dehydration, she didn't have the typical symptomology of Agent X.

"What are the doctors saying?" Sam asked.

"They're saying I have to stay here until they figure out what I have. They haven't taken my blood, though, so I don't know how they're supposed to figure it out without that."

"This... agent that they think you might have, it's really infectious, and most hospital staff won't go near a patient. They probably have a policy that they won't do blood draws on suspected cases."

"How long will they keep me here?"

Samantha glanced at Duncan and then looked at her sister. "There's some things going on in the city that you may not have heard about, Jane. Communications have been cut off, and they've begun containment centers."

"I was in one of the centers. Robert and his family went down to San Diego for the zoo. I was here alone. They said if I took a potential vaccine, I could go home."

"I know."

"What do you mean they've shut down the city, though?"

"Everything's off. No cars on the road, no one at work, nothing. They're frightened of this pathogen getting out."

"Who's *they*?"

"The military, the NSA. Probably the FBI and CIA, too. Whoever does this sort of thing. They've decided we're a disaster zone and declared martial law."

Jane turned away, and staring up at the ceiling, she shook her head. "I don't believe this."

Samantha rose. "Duncan, wait for me here."

"Where you going?"

"I'm going to take a blood sample and have it tested. If she's clear, I'm getting her out of here."

35

The car slowed down on a residential street in Van Nuys. The homes were immaculate, and from the cars in the driveways, Katherine could tell this was an affluent neighborhood. A white house with a sports car and an SUV in the driveway came into view on the right, and Ian instructed her to stop there.

"He's asleep," she said. "They probably have an alarm, too."

"Who's the alarm going to call?" He grinned, took the keys out of the ignition, and put them in his pocket. "Stay here. You're doing really well, Katherine. This will all be over soon."

Ian got out of the car, and she watched as he walked around the house, checking the windows. He was limping, and she realized he had hurt himself during the accident, too, but he didn't let it bother him. He disappeared around the back. She glanced around the neighborhood. She wasn't aware of the time, other than it was well after midnight, and the clock on the dash was blinking 12:00. The neighborhood seemed darker than any she had ever been in. Not a single light was on in any house. She opened the door and felt the warmth of the night. She debated no more than a few seconds, and then she ran down the street as fast as she could.

The sidewalk was clean, and running wasn't difficult, except for the fact that she was still lightheaded from the pain medication in her system. But it wasn't enough to affect her balance.

She was halfway down the block when she turned down a side street and then another and another. She was going to get lost and disappear in the maze of homes. One house had an open gate. Glancing around, she didn't see a dog. Once inside, she shut the door behind her and then sat down. She hoped she could sit there until morning. If she had entered the house and sought the help of the people inside, Ian would see the lights on. She had to wait until morning and then hope she could get in touch with the police.

As she sat, she realized she was really hungry and thirsty. In the hospital, she was in shock and couldn't think clearly enough to ask for something, and she regretted that right then.

She thought about her mother's apple pie. Every last Sunday of the month, her mother made fresh apple pie with peach-apples, a type of apple mixed with a peach grown by a local farmer. They were a bit softer and sweeter than normal apples and had a tanginess she'd never tasted in anything else. Her mother made her pies with brown sugar and then scooped vanilla ice cream on top while the pie was still hot, and they would eat on the porch or in the backyard.

When her mother passed away from the brain tumor, Katherine had tried to make the pie for her two sisters, her brother, and her father, but it always turned out either too crisp or too soggy. No one enjoyed it, but Katherine wouldn't stop making it. She got up early once a month to go to the farmer's market for a batch of peach-apples and then started the pie from scratch.

Brakes squealed behind her. They weren't loud, like someone was going fast and then had to quickly stop, but they built up in pitch, as if someone were going slowly and had rolled by in front of the house where she was hiding.

She didn't move or even breathe. Keeping entirely still, she felt a tickling on her leg. Glancing down at her ankle, she saw a spider the size of a quarter resting on it.

Katherine put her hand over her mouth to make sure she didn't scream. The spider crawled again, and instead of going over, it went up her leg. She bit down hard on her lip and closed her eyes. Squealing, she swatted at her ankle and then opened her eyes to see the spider was gone.

The car revved its engine and then drove away.

Katherine jumped to her feet and opened the gate. She didn't see anyone. She sprinted to the middle of the road, but couldn't see the car anymore. As she was about to run up to the house where she'd been hiding, she stopped. What exactly could they do for her? The phones had been cut off, and no police were available. Who would come and help her?

But at least she would be away from him. She walked up to the porch and knocked on the door. She got no answer at first, and so she rang the doorbell and then knocked again. A light went on inside the house, and then another. A middle-aged man in a black robe opened the door. Behind him, peeking out over his shoulder, was a beautiful blonde with large, fake breasts.

"Please," Katherine said, "I'm in tr—"

The blood spattered on her face. She felt numb as the man's corpse collapsed backward into his wife, who hadn't even realized what had happened yet. Blood and gore was all over her nightgown and her chest, and as the body fell, she caught it and brought it down. When she saw the gaping hole in his head, she screamed.

"No!"

Katherine quietly took in the scene. It didn't seem real to her, as if it were happening to someone else far away and she were only watching, like a waking dream. She turned, and Ian was in the street.

Katherine's mind was reeling. In one moment of absolute, pure rage, she felt out of control. She ran out into the street and shouted, "You want to kill me? Then fucking kill me!"

He lifted his weapon, and she thought she was going to die. But she didn't care. Right then, she was helping a man who was little more than an animal and was worried that God would judge her for it. She thought it better to die. She lifted her arms and closed her eyes, waiting for the bullet to tear into her. But it never came.

She opened her eyes as Ian slammed the butt of the gun against her jaw, knocking her out cold.

36

Samantha put on latex gloves and a full biohazard suit. She combed the supply closet for sodium hypochlorite and found some tucked away on a shelf. She also found a syringe and vial for testing as well as some swabs and a small packet of alcohol.

She stripped down to her bra and panties and then slipped the blue suit over herself. The plastic faceplate was free of any smudges or fingerprints. It was brand-new.

Placing the boots on her feet, she realized they were too large. She tried cinching them with rubber bands. They were still loose, but would have to do.

She slipped the crinkly booties over her boots and then pulled on the suit's thick black gloves and tucked her sleeves into them. Taking a deep breath, she closed her eyes for a moment before opening them and going out into the corridor.

Duncan was standing outside the room. He seemed to want to say something but didn't. Maybe because he knew she was going to do it no matter what, or maybe because he, too, thought it was the right thing.

"Where are the Rangers?" she asked.

"I called Clyde and had them reassigned. You're clear for a few hours until they send some others."

Sam was silent a moment. "Thanks," she finally said.

"You're welcome."

"Find a coffee for me, will ya?" She didn't want one, but she knew it might occupy his mind long enough for her to get the blood. Entering the room, she shut the door behind her, then tore off the tape on the floor that was holding down the canopy.

Slipping underneath, she came up next to her sister and placed her hand on her shoulder. Jane gave her a weak smile and placed her hand over the glove.

Sam swabbed her sister's left bicep with a cotton swab and alcohol.

"Close your eyes," she said.

"You still remember, huh?" Jane said.

Samantha thought back to a doctor's office they had been in when she was twelve and Jane eight. The doctor needed to give her vaccinations, and Jane sprinted out of the room and ran into the parking lot. Their father had to chase her and bring her back. Holding her down, they finally got the injection in by telling her to close her eyes, and Jane passed out.

"What do you do when they have to give you an IV?" Sam asked.

"They've never had to. I avoid the damn things as much as possible."

Sam withdrew a vial of the black-red blood, and it splashed up as it filled the tube. She capped and sealed it, then ducked under the canopy and went over to a sink. She washed both the bag and the vial of blood with water and then the sodium hypochlorite. She placed the vial in the bag and threw the syringe into a biohazard trash bin.

"I'll be right back," Sam said.

No showers were set up for decontamination, so Sam had to use the one in the room. When she finished washing the suit, she stepped out and went to the supply closet to get dressed.

The hematology department was on a different floor, and she carefully carried the plastic container in both hands as she went to the elevators. A custodian was on there with her, and he was humming to himself. It seemed so out of place for the moment that Sam couldn't help but watch him. He smiled at her as he stepped off onto his floor.

Hematology was empty up front. Sam walked behind the front desk and toward the back. Sitting at a table with various vials, tubes, and microscopes set up in front of him was a man with orange hair and a goatee. He was writing on a notepad, and Sam walked in and placed the plastic bag down on the table.

"You need to test this," she said. "For an unknown pathogen resembling smallpox."

The man was confused for a second, and then his eyes widened. "Holy shit, you brought that here like that?"

"Test it now, please. I'll be back in a couple of hours."

"There's different kinds of smallpox virion, and most are morphologically indistinguishable from the others. I can't tell you what I'd be looking at."

"You have to do negative staining. Do you have an electron microscope here?"

"Well, yeah, but I would need some sort of scab or skin sample from an infected patient to do it."

"You have two people infected upstairs. I'll get you the skin sample. You just get everything ready."

As she was walking out, the doctor said, "Hey, who the hell are you anyway?"

"I'm with the CDC… and I'm that patient's sister."

37

After speeding away in the jeep, Howie was going so fast that he nearly lost control and tipped over on a sharp turn. He slowed down and noticed the sky. No choppers. He glanced to his daughter in the passenger seat and saw that her hand was on his knee.

"You okay?" he said.

"Yeah. Mike looked after me."

Howie glimpsed in the rearview. "Thanks," he said.

"No problem."

After driving in silence for a few more minutes, Howie realized he was hungry. An Italian place called Cosimo's was up near the intersection, and he pulled around back and parked in the handicap section.

"I don't think they'll mind," he said, looking at his daughter.

"What're we doing here?" Mike said.

"You guys hungry?"

"Starving."

"Let's go. I'll whip something up."

The restaurant was open. They walked in through the front door, and Jessica went to turn on the lights, but Howie told her not to. They would have to eat in the dark.

"See if you can find some candles, though," he said.

Walking to the kitchen, Howie saw food still out on the tables. A dish of gelato had melted and was soaking the tablecloth. Everyone had gotten out of there in a hurry.

Mike came with him as Jessica lagged behind. The lights in the kitchen as well as the grill and oven were still on. He turned them off and went to the fridge on the other side of the room. Taking out some beef, pasta, and vegetables, he then found the olive oil and cooked macaroni with sauce.

Mike stood in the corner and chewed on some bread with butter. "Where we heading?"

"I don't know. I was thinking out of the state. See if whatever's happening here is happening there, too."

"I heard all the highways are closed. How you planning on getting out?"

"We got a jeep. We'll fill her up and try the desert."

"You want to risk driving through the desert on one tank of gas?"

"I don't know what to do, Mike. I've never been in this situation before. If you got a better idea, by all means, share."

Mike took another bite of the bread. "I was in Iraq."

"I didn't know that."

"No, you wouldn't. We had taken this small town, called Karim. The insurgents, that's what we were forced to call them, they had taken the town, and we got it back. It took four days. Two days of no sleep. Some o' the guys took amphetamines to stay awake, and it did things to their minds. No sleep and drugs aren't the best solution to anything, but we were young. So we take the town. And we decide we don't know who's with them and who's with us, so we impose a curfew and patrol the streets. Anyone suspected of working with the insurgents was rounded up, and we turned this mosque into like a camp for them.

"At first, the people were happy. They hated the insurgents more than we did. One guy told me they were all Arabians, and what the fuck did he care about Arabians. But after a while, we started acting… different. I don't know what it is or why it happens, but once you got power over someone, you start treating 'em different. Like they ain't even human. A lot of horrible things started happenin', especially with the women."

He swallowed and placed the bread down on the counter. His eyes were lost, staring into nothing as he spoke, and Howie didn't interrupt him.

"So after a little bit, the people started fighting us. They thought they'd just exchanged one conquering army for another. And that's when the suicide bombings started. We took an entire village that loved us and made it so they would rather blow themselves up than live with us. That's what happens. That's what'll happen here, and lots of people are going to get killed."

Howie didn't say anything for a while as he coated a pan in olive oil, and then he turned to the stove and fired it up. He didn't know what to say, so he cooked instead, and Mike went to another fridge down a hallway.

Howie watched Mike go to a metal door with a lock on it, and he searched for something to break it open with. After finding a hammer and other tools in a box, he slammed the hammer into the lock until it clinked to the ground. The fridge was a walk-in and he found some beer and brought out six bottles, placing them on the counter. He popped open the first one and took a long drink.

"Better give me one of those too," Howie said.

38

Katherine only remembered pain against her jaw and then a headache. Next thing she knew, she was in the Audi, and Ian was sitting in the passenger seat. He opened a sports drink.

"Here," he said, handing her the bottle.

She drank the warm drink without protest. After swigging half of it, she stopped to wipe her lips with the palm of her hand. Ian took the bottle and drank some before replacing the lid and putting it on the floor between his feet.

"You feel okay?" he asked.

She nodded but didn't say anything.

"I need you to drive," he said.

"Drive yourself."

"I can't. I've injured my leg, and it's starting not to respond. I need you to drive. There's just two more."

"Do you even care that they had a family? That they're the ones that are going to find them? I know what that will do to their kids. They won't ever be the same."

"How do you know that?"

"My mother died of cancer. When she finally passed, I was the one in the hospital with her. She couldn't talk, but she was trying to say goodbye to me." She held his gaze. "You think taking lives is a game, but I think you're scared. I think you're scared that you're going to die one day, too."

He didn't react but instead watched the landscape through the windshield. They were in a residential neighborhood, and a car stopped in front of one of the houses. A teenage boy of maybe sixteen stepped out and went to the front door. He carefully placed his key in the lock and opened the door, stopping for a moment to see if anyone heard him. Then he went inside and shut the door behind him.

"When I first killed someone, I was so scared, I pissed myself. I mean, I literally pissed my pants. I still remember how warm it was going down my leg. I was in Moscow at the time, and it was freezing, but I remember the comforting feeling of how warm it was. After it was done, I went back to the little room I'd been staying at and cried. I actually fucking cried. Like a little girl that had lost her puppy. It tore me up for a long time. But after the second one, I didn't cry. I thought I should, and I wanted the tears to come, but they never did. I couldn't do it. By the fifth one, it didn't feel like anything anymore. And now… it's actually fun. It's probably the only fun I have left in my life."

"Well, then I feel sorry for you."

He took a deep breath, staring off into space. "Start the car."

"No."

He was quiet for a second. "I said, start the car."

"You'll have to kill me. I'm not helping you anymore."

"I won't kill you," he said. "I told you I wouldn't, so I'd stick to my word. But I will kill your father. And then your sisters and your brother. Any man you ever love will one day disappear, and you won't know if it was because they left you or because I paid them a visit. You'll live the rest of your life with me hanging over your shoulder, and you'll never really know if I'm there or not. Now turn on the fucking car."

She sat still. No more tears were left. Her emotions were so frayed that she couldn't even bring up enough passion to plead with him. She turned on the car.

"Who's the next one?" she said.

"A doctor. Samantha Bower."

39

The hospital was as still as a museum after hours. No one spoke, the televisions were all off, and the radio, walkie-talkies, and cell phones were silent. Many of the staff, a nurse had told Samantha, had simply left without clocking out or letting their supervisors know. Something was wrong, and everybody knew it, so they wanted to be with their families. Only a handful of the staff remained, including maybe a dozen doctors. Samantha sat outside hematology to ensure that the doctor running her sister's negative staining test was one of them.

Duncan had fallen asleep on the chairs in the waiting area. He spread out over three of them without armrests, and Sam had unplugged the television to ensure he didn't wake up. His eyes had black circles underneath them. He wasn't as used to sleep deprivation as she was.

She went down to the vending machines and got a Diet Coke and a small bag of peanuts. Going back to hematology, she took the long route around the corridor to get blood back into her legs. Hospitals all seemed as though they had been designed and decorated by the same person. The linoleum was spotless in parts and as filthy as mud in others. Antiseptic smells mingled with cleaning products and lifeless, sour air. And they all used lighting that, in a certain percentage of the population, caused migraines.

She had always noticed that they weren't comforting, and she wondered why that was. Maybe the association with them was so strongly negative that no decorations could ever overcome it. People, of course, only came there when bad things happened. The only exception was childbirth.

For a time during her medical school rotations, she'd thought about going into obstetrics, but pathology and trauma had called to her. When she had joined the CDC, something about it seemed so thrilling, so cutting edge. There she was, hardly out of medical school, and she was in a village in Chad performing an emergency surgery on someone whose gallbladder had ruptured. Initially, she had gone there to investigate a water-supply contaminate.

Samantha discovered the source of the contamination was a single well rumored to contain the feces of some children that had defecated in it as a practical joke, causing an E. coli outbreak. She was the only doctor within two hundred miles. A man suffering from poor hydration and malnutrition had drunk from the well, and the E. coli infected his gallbladder and caused it to rupture.

The village elders had begged her to perform the surgery, and she'd spent just enough time as an emergency room physician and surgeon to operate without killing the man.

She removed the gallbladder and closed the incisions, hoping that no sepsis would occur. The man was rushed 211 miles to the nearest hospital for follow-up care and antibiotics. Sam found out later that the man had survived. He even sent her some homemade trinkets, including a giraffe carved out of yellow wood.

Now, she wasn't certain that joining the CDC had been the right decision. But she knew the history of infections was the history of the world, and sometimes, she felt there was no greater calling in medicine than to stop the spread of disease.

Microorganisms were responsible for the shaping of antiquity. People thought that history had variables that could be rearranged to predict with some accuracy how history flowed. One country falls to dictatorship, and a certain result follows. Another country inflates its currency, and a specific result was expected. But Samantha knew that wasn't true. Humans had always been at the mercy of beings too small to see them, except through powerful instruments.

The Emperor of the Byzantine Empire, Justinian the First, had the misfortune of being attributed with the worst plague in history. He expanded the reach of the Byzantine Empire, and by all historical predictions, the Byzantines should have conquered the known world, much as the Romans had. But a simple plague brought the empire to its knees and halted expansion, which allowed the Muslim nations to grow stronger.

The Mongols used to infect their enemies with Plague by catapulting infected persons over the gates of cities they had besieged. The cities would surrender, then the Mongols destroyed them and enslaved their people. Hundreds of cities were conquered this way, and entire nations had been forced to change the way they traded and conducted their politics and economics, based on avoiding confrontation with the Mongols.

And the Black Plague of Europe forever changed the balance of power between the great nations, causing, in some way, everything that came after it in Europe and consequently affecting every territory under the British crown.

People were the slaves of bugs a million times smaller than particles of dust.

And the worst of them was the poxvirus, which was so deadly and contagious that humanity worked to abolish it. Humans understood they could not co-exist while this virus was still alive in nature. But it had returned and had become unlike anything anyone had seen. Samantha estimated that it had a 99.9998 percent mortality rate. She knew of only one person who had survived infection, but she had been so badly scarred by the virus that she was blind, deaf, and unable to walk because the infection had destroyed her nerves and blood vessels. Sam would rather have died.

The door to hematology opened, and the young doctor stood there, his safety goggles pushed up onto his forehead. He handed a printout to Samantha.

40

Lt. General Clyde Olsen sat in a hard plastic chair inside the medical trailer and watched as several of his men communicated with bases across the state. More cases of the poxvirus were being reported, and he didn't know how that had occurred. Everyone with symptoms had been hospitalized. The only explanation was that some people hadn't gone to the hospital, but they would all be dead long ago. They wouldn't have had a chance to infect many others. But the numbers he was getting were off the charts. Some people, somehow, had escaped.

Ten reported cases in Sacramento, twelve in San Francisco, thirteen in Los Angeles, six in Oakland—the list went on and on. He was losing control of this thing. At least the state was locked down. None of these people would be going anywhere.

The phone rang. A private line was connected to his desk in the trailer. He picked it up and said hello.

"Clyde, it's Lancaster. What the hell's going on out there?"

"We've hit a bit of a snag, sir. Just a minor setback."

"The reports I'm getting are saying there's over seventy new reported cases up and down the state."

"That sounds about right."

"So what the fuck happened?"

"Frankly sir, what we all suspected would. The pathogen got out somehow. Unless some people either couldn't or wouldn't admit themselves to the hospital and continued the spread, this thing escaped under our watch."

"Damn fucking hippie nature loving cocksuckers…"

Clyde didn't respond and waited until General Lancaster finished swearing. He cursed for a good ten seconds before calming down and leaving silence between them.

"Get it locked down. Now."

"Yes, sir. And one more thing, sir."

"Yeah."

"There's some concern that if the infected are still among the gen pop, they could cause an outbreak within the containment facilities."

"Yeah, and?"

He was silent for a moment, shocked by Lancaster's statement. "And there are thousands of people there, sir. Including our own men. They'd be like cows in a slaughterhouse."

"Exactly, *confined* to a slaughterhouse."

"You can't be serious."

"Clyde, you think I like this decision? You think this is a fucking good time for me? It tears my guts out to make these calls, but someone has to make them. Our top priority is to contain that virus. We cannot allow it into any other state. Do you understand that, Clyde? Nothing else matters."

"Yes, sir. I understand."

"Good. Now, for these new cases, the hospitals will probably be overwhelmed soon. Create another facility for use only for the infected. No one else can be admitted there. Have anyone watching them in full biohazard gear. No accidents."

"Yes, sir. It'll get done."

"I know it will."

41

Ian sat in the passenger seat of the Audi and tested his knee. He placed his left foot over his right and pressed down. Then he lifted the leg at the back of his injured knee. The lower part of his leg separated about two inches. Nothing was holding it in place.

"So other than delivering meals to the homeless," he said, "what do you plan to do with your life?"

"I wanted to be an environmentalist. Work at a non-profit, something like that."

"What for?"

She kept her eyes on the road. "Someone like you wouldn't understand."

"Someone like me?"

"You don't care about anything but yourself."

"Probably true, but let me tell you a little secret about your Mother Earth. She doesn't care about anything but herself, either. She's constantly trying to kill us with earthquakes and volcanoes and tsunamis and disease... She's not our friend, and she's not in need of saving. If I stripped you naked and dropped you anywhere over ninety percent of this planet, you would be dead within one day." He twisted his injured knee to the side, and a sharp pain shot up his leg.

"The earth is apathetic," she said. "It's not malicious."

"Surveys were done in 1904 in New York, asking people what they were scared of. The number one thing was black lung, tuberculosis, and number two was famine. They didn't mention viruses or asteroids or heart disease or car accidents because they didn't know about them. Now think a century from now what knowledge we'll have and what the answers would be to the same survey. It'll be things we don't even know about. That's nature. It runs on death. If anything, I'm more in tune with it than you are."

Ian pulled out his phone and checked his list. There had been an update on this one. Samantha Bower was initially last on his list since he was going to fly back to Atlanta, where she lived, once everyone in California had been taken care of. But the update stated that she was in Los Angeles.

"What did this doctor do?" she asked.

"I told you, it's nothing they've done. It's what they will do."

"That doesn't seem fair."

"Fair? What are you, six years old? Haven't you learned that lesson yet?"

She spent most of the ride in silence. Occasionally, Ian asked her questions, which she answered with only single sentences or yes and no. He eventually stopped trying and stared out the window.

He knew Los Angeles well. It was all glimmer and shine on the surface, but underneath was a dark heart that beat in harmony with the worst aspects of men. The city's essence was one of use—everyone was used by someone else. And the city never seemed to run out of people. So it had an endless supply of people to drain and discard. The vampire city, his father had called it when Ian told him he was moving back there after his stint in the military.

"I lived here once," he said, not taking his eyes off the passing landscape before him. "Twice, actually. First, maybe fifteen years ago, when I was a young kid. I saw a man get shot in the middle of the sidewalk during the day. At least a dozen people saw it. The person closest to him as he died on the cement looked at him less than five seconds before stepping over him… I've never forgotten that. They'll all step over you in the end, Katherine. Everyone."

She glanced over, and he was fidgeting with a small statue of Saint Cyril in his hand. "What is that?"

He glared at her and, for a moment, forgot who she was. Then he remembered and put the trinket back into his pocket. "Nothing. She's supposed to be at the hospital up here. Stop in front and wait for me."

42

After their meal, which was eaten by candlelight, Howie, his daughter, and Mike got back into the jeep. The streets seemed quieter than before. Maybe because the moon was tucked away behind the clouds. He'd always noticed that people were louder when the moon was full. He was glad it wasn't full that night.

They drove through Malibu, to Thousand Oaks, and then up through Bakersfield. The farther they drove from Malibu, the fewer choppers were in the distance. Howie drove near Interstate 5, where he saw nothing but normal vehicles. A couple of roadblocks were up, but if you knew the area they were easy to avoid. *Didn't do your research before coming here, did you bastards?* Howie thought.

"They didn't quarantine up here," Mike said. "Why would they just do Malibu?"

Howie didn't respond. He was busy trying to find a way back onto the interstate. When he came across an entrance that was blocked by signs indicating the onramp was being repaired, he ignored them and drove up. He didn't see any damage anywhere.

"Where you going?" Mike asked.

"Up through Nipton and into Las Vegas. And then as far away from here as I can get."

"I don't know anyone in Vegas. Do you?"

"No. But I have a brother in Seattle. Maybe we'll go out there after and figure out what the hell is going on."

The city disappeared behind them a short while later, and they were on I-15, heading through the desert near Joshua Tree National Park. The dunes and rock formations were interspersed with patches of forest, and he stopped outside one at a gas station. People were getting gas and snacks like they would on any normal day. Howie watched them and felt sorry for them. In a moment of fear that was coming, when they heard a pounding on the door, they would comprehend they were helpless to stop it. And it would terrify them.

They walked around and stretched their legs, and Howie realized he didn't have any money to pay for gas.

"What're we gonna do?" Mike said. "It's pay first."

Just behind them, a man pulled up in a silver BMW and got out. He swiped his card and put the nozzle into the tank, then went around to the side of his car to check for scratches while the tank filled. Howie looked to Mike.

"We have to do it," Howie said.

"Beat up some innocent guy and take his wallet?"

"Yes."

"I'm not doing that."

Howie thought of his daughter. "We need to get over the state line. We're in trouble, Mike."

"Let me handle it."

Mike walked over to the man, "Hey, you're not going to believe this, but both of us forgot our wallets. I promise you we will send down a check if you could help us out right now and fill up our tank. We're in really—"

"Fuck off, asshole," the man said as he came around the car and finished his exterior check. As he passed Howie, he grimaced.

As soon as he was turned around, Howie wrapped his arm around the man's throat. He took him down to the ground as Mike grabbed his legs.

Howie reached into the man's pants and took out his wallet. He flung it to Mike. "Fill up the fucking tank!"

The man was struggling, and Howie had to get on top of him to hold him down. He got hit in the face twice before he got his knees around the guy's ribs and was able to hold his arms down at the elbows.

"Get the fuck off me!"

"Sorry. We need to do this."

The man was grunting and writhing around like a wild boar. Mike filled the tank, glancing into the gas station to see if anyone was seeing this.

"It's full," Mike said as he climbed in.

"Don't follow us."

Howie got up and jumped into the jeep. The man in the rearview ran to his car. He reached into his glove compartment and came out with a pistol.

"Shit!"

He grabbed Jessica's head and pushed her down to the floor of the jeep as the first shot nearly shattered their windshield. He slammed on the gas and peeled away as the pop of gunfire went off behind them.

The man and his pistol chased them only a dozen feet or so as Howie sped down the dark highway.

43

Samantha froze. She didn't take the test results out of the hematologist's hands for a moment, and the doctor pushed it closer to her. She lifted it and read the page.

Negative.

She let out a sigh and felt weak. The results fell out of her hand, and the doctor appeared perplexed. He bent down and picked it up, then returned to the lab before she could thank him. She stood staring at the door, unable to speak, until Duncan roused behind her.

"What'd he say?"

"Negative," she said after a long pause.

"Wow. Thank the Lord," he said.

"I don't think the Lord has anything to do with this, Duncan."

She turned away and collapsed in the chair next to him. Every muscle ached, and her entire body was pulling at her to sleep. Though she'd been only a day without sleep, she felt as if she could pass out at any moment. Her eyelids drooped, and her mind was a slushy mess.

"Probably a reaction to the weakened virus," Duncan said. "We need to run the blood for antibodies and see if she's developed immunities."

Sam nodded. "I need to sleep."

"Do you want to get her out?"

"Not yet. Until she recovers, she's probably the safest here."

"They'd booked a hotel for us. You wanna go back there?"

"Yeah. Lemme say bye to her and let her know. Can you call Olsen and have him pick up the blood for testing?"

"Sure."

Duncan headed downstairs as Sam went back to the quarantine zone. She opened her sister's door, and Jane was asleep in the darkness, a slight snore escaping her lips. Sam woke her softly and told her the news. They both cried and held each other.

Deciding to take the stairs to help wake up, Sam felt her legs more acutely than she had in a long time. She felt almost as if they were letting her know they were about to abandon her, and she could no longer rely on them. She placed her hand on the banister for balance.

As she headed downstairs, she heard the swoosh of papers flying onto the floor and then the thump of something heavy hitting the linoleum. Down the corridor, a man in a pinstripe suit stood over the body of a hospital security guard. Behind the desk, a nurse was leaning far back in a chair, a single hole in her forehead; blood oozed out and down her temples.

The shooter kicked the officer to make sure the man was dead, and then his head came up, and her eyes met his.

She didn't know how she knew, but she did. He was there for her.

As she darted up the stairs, two slugs embedded into the wall where she had been standing, spitting drywall and dust into her face. She pushed her legs as hard as they would go, but she felt as though she were running through sand. Another shot rang in her ears as the round bounced off the metal railing and ricocheted somewhere below.

She opened the first door she came across and ran down a corridor with patient rooms on either side. She sprinted past a nurse's station, where a single nurse was sitting behind a computer. The nurse yelled something to her, but Sam couldn't hear.

Sam turned to her, still running, and shouted, "There's a man with a gun!" She couldn't think of anything else to say that would convey the urgency of the moment. But she ran a bit, and when she glanced back, the nurse hadn't moved. The door at the end of the corridor opened, and the shooter stepped through.

Sam ran to the elevators and pushed all the buttons. Out of breath, with panic slowly closing in around her, she wasn't there. She was back in her house with a man named Greyjoy standing above her, telling her she was about to die. Samantha felt as though she were breathing through a towel.

One shot, nothing more than a spit, sounded like a plastic cup falling onto linoleum. It zipped past her, close enough that she sensed the wind from the shot. The round exploded the window behind her as one of the elevators opened, and she jumped on. The shooter chased her at a full sprint.

She pounded the button for the top floor, her injured arm aching beneath the cast, and the doors slowly closed as the man leapt to get his hand in between them. The pull of gravity made her stomach roil as the elevator lifted her higher into the building.

44

With no streetlights and a moon that seemed to be hiding from them, Howie had no means to see anything other than the headlights on the jeep. He felt surrounded by a great black nothingness, but the headlights made it appear as though they were barreling through a light tunnel. Jessica was asleep, and he reached over and moved a strand of hair out of her face that was whipping her skin.

"She told me about you," Mike said, leaning behind his ear from the backseat.

"What'd she say?"

"She said you cheated on her mom and got divorced after."

Howie glanced into the rearview mirror. "It was… I don't know. I don't even know. I put myself in a spot I shouldn't have, and I couldn't resist. The only way to avoid it is to not even be in a place where you can fumble."

"We're weak when it comes to that stuff," Mike said. "You still with the woman you cheated with?"

"No. It was a one-time thing. My wife only found out about it because she saw a package of condoms in my car. I tried to cover for it, but she could tell I was lying." He paused. "She sat in her room from sunup to sundown and cried. Didn't eat, didn't drink. She cried the entire day."

"That's fucked up."

"Yeah."

"Maybe it was for the best?"

"No, it wasn't. I screwed up the best thing in my life real good. And you don't even realize it until later. I saw it tonight when she hugged my leg. I felt a glimpse of what I was missing out on. No amount of pussy is worth that."

The state line wasn't far. Excitement tingled Howie's belly, and the stars were even beginning to sparkle above them, providing a dim light. A tinge of morning was in the warm air, which wasn't as warm as it had been a couple of hours before.

"Daddy?"

"What is it, sweetheart?"

"Your nose is bleeding."

He checked his nose in the mirror. Sweat glistened on his face, and underneath his nostrils a thread of blood was pooling at his upper lip. He wiped it with the back of his sleeve.

"It's nothing, sweetheart. Just the dry air."

She didn't move for a time, though he could tell she wanted to hug him. But her anger wouldn't let her. She had so much of it that she was blinded to everything else. He put his hand over her shoulders, careful to touch only her clothing. But that made him uncomfortable, and he withdrew his hand and put them both on the steering wheel.

"Go back to sleep, Jess. We'll be in Las Vegas soon, and we'll get a hotel room there and a big breakfast."

"Can I have coffee and a waffle?"

"Whatever you want."

He glanced over at her, and she smiled as an explosion rang in his ears and the jeep spun nearly upside down, gliding through the air like a monstrous bird.

Howie put his arm against Jessica to prevent her from flying out, but her seat belt held her in place. Mike wasn't wearing one. He flew out of the jeep and rolled on the ground, narrowly missing the ton of steel that came crashing into the earth.

The jeep rolled once, groaning to an upright position. The motion jarred Howie's neck, and a wave of pain shot into his head.

When it had straightened out, he turned to Jessica, who was crying. He put his arms around her and told her that it was all right, that they must have hit a batch of rocks. A trail of blood dribbled onto his sleeve and into her hair. He frantically wiped it out of her hair with his hands and then the sleeves of his shirt.

"What're you doing, Dad?"

He didn't respond. Terror gripped him, and he wiped at her face and hands until she pushed him away.

"Stop it. Stop!"

He sat back, breathing heavily. His acute anxiety was causing his chest to tighten like a walnut about to be cracked. They sat staring at each other for a moment before he realized that an acrid smell was filling the air. He glanced at the engine and saw flames.

Howie tugged at Jessica's seat belt, but it wouldn't loosen. He reached down and tried to unclip it, but the metal clip was jammed and the button wouldn't depress. He felt the hilt of the knife he'd stolen earlier pushing into his abdomen. He pulled it out and cut through the belt. But before he could pull her out, a noise startled him.

The flames blew the hood off the jeep and reached into the front seats.

45

Samantha leapt out of the elevator, unsure of what floor she was on. A flood of memories of the past month overtook her senses so profoundly that she thought she might faint. But she kept running. Not until she was standing at the windows, staring down at the parking lot, did she know she had arrived at the top floor.

She ran into one of the rooms and shut the door behind her. Then she ran to the bathroom and shut that door. Samantha stared at it as though it would explode off its hinges at any moment. She backed away and sat on the toilet, nearly falling off. Putting her hands to her face, she sobbed.

After a few moments, the emotions passed. She took a deep breath and thought about what to do next.

Duncan and Jane were downstairs, and Samantha couldn't be certain that man didn't know about them. She didn't know how to help either of them. Robert Greyjoy had known everything about her before they had even met.

She stood up and walked to the door. The shooter had come for her. She didn't understand why she knew that, but she could read the unspoken understanding between them, like a crackling energy. He was the hunter, and she was the hunted. Maybe if he killed her, he would leave Jane and Duncan alone.

She opened the door, stood there a moment with her eyes closed, and stepped out into the room.

A woman was in the bed. Her closed eyes were turned toward the window, and a beeping monitor echoed in the small space. Samantha walked to the bed. The woman's face was wrinkled and gray.

Samantha wasn't sure how long she stood there, but eventually, she sat down in a chair against the wall. The woman's hair was thin and missing in spots. She seemed so weak and fragile that death couldn't have been far off. Tears swirled in Samantha's eyes, but she didn't wipe them away. Instead, she put her hand over the woman's and sat quietly, listening to the rhythmic beep of the machine and the deep, grainy breaths that the woman pulled into her thin body.

Finally, Sam rose and walked out into the corridor. She shut the door softly, then glanced down both directions before walking to the front desk. She wasn't going to run anymore. She didn't see a point to running. If he was like Greyjoy, he would catch up with her.

She quickly jumped on the elevator and went down to her floor.

When she got off, the floor was empty and quiet. She went into Jane's room, and there, standing next to the canopy, was the shooter. His weapon hung at his side between relaxed fingers.

"I knew you'd come here," he said.

"What do you want?"

"I want you to die."

She shivered and averted her eyes, turning them to Jane. "What about her?"

"Make it easy, and she lives."

Samantha nodded. Ian raised his weapon, aiming for her heart.

46

He didn't have much sensation at first, just a general numbness and anxiety. As Howie Burke took his daughter in his arms, he grasped that he shouldn't be holding her and withdrew. The jeep was upright but severely damaged. He sat up, ignoring the pain in his back and arms, and he thought about trying to start the vehicle but decided against it.

The fire was rising over the seat at a steady but slow pace. He pulled Jessica away from the vehicle.

He heard tires in dirt and the shouting of men. Headlights swarming them, he impotently watched the terror in his daughter's eyes. He had no words of comfort for her or explanations. Instead, he turned away from her and saw Mike a little behind them. His head had been crushed so thoroughly that it was only a slick in the dark, a black puddle in front of a fully-grown male body.

"Who are they?" Jessica asked.

Howie watched the jeeps. Five of them roared to a stop near them, and men in uniforms jumped out, pointing terrifying black weapons at them. They shouted orders, but Howie couldn't hear them. He couldn't hear anything but a soft buzzing sound, and he wondered if Jessica had really spoken or if he'd imagined it.

The men were closing in around them, their lips moving, their faces contorted with rage and fear. One of them was young, maybe eighteen. He was trembling and sweating, and in the headlights of the jeep, Howie saw that his fingers were turning white from gripping his rifle too hard.

Other men were next to Howie, closer than the boy. But Howie saw only him. They were on the same frequency somehow. The two of them knew what was about to happen; this incident was between them, and everyone else was just there to witness it.

Neither of them averted their eyes as they stared into each other. The soldier's eyes were wide, and he didn't blink, despite the droplets of sweat rolling into them.

And in an instant, both their lives changed.

"Run, Jessica!"

Howie sprinted. The first soldier was only a couple feet away, and Howie grabbed his rifle and kicked the soldier in the chest, sending him to the dirt. The other soldier swung at him, but Howie tackled him before the butt of the rifle impacted his face. He slammed his fist into the soldier's jaw, but the soldier barely seemed to notice.

The young soldier, horror written on his face, aimed the rifle. His hands trembling worse than before, he fired a single shot, and Howie was suddenly staring up at the sky without any memory of the motion that had put him there.

He lay helplessly on his back as two soldiers slapped handcuffs on Jessica. He screamed for her but couldn't hear the words that came out of his mouth.

47

Carrie Mendelsohn had been feeling unwell for over twenty-four hours. A slight fever, alternating with cold sweats and shivering, had been burning away in her, and her skin was sensitive to almost everything. Even wearing clothing made her itch until she had scratched her skin raw. Her throat hurt, and her stomach felt as if it were about to shoot vomit out of her any second.

She sat by the outdoor pool at the Monte Carlo Hotel, thinking that maybe cooling off in the water would help. She rose and went to the pool. Her swimsuit was rolled up too far on her thighs, revealing the bottoms of her buttocks. As she went into the water, she pulled her suit down to cover herself, though she hardly cared, considering that some of the people there were almost topless. She floated around, kicked a few times, and then lay back and closed her eyes. The water was warmer than she'd thought it would be, and she dipped beneath the surface, then came up, slicking her hair back with both hands. The water in front of her was discolored.

Her nose was bleeding. At least a hundred people were in the pool, and she was so embarrassed, she quickly jumped out and ran to her pool chair, where she toweled off before going inside.

Her sorority had booked a room on the sixth floor, overlooking the strip. She swiped her card and went inside. Her clothes were all over the room, interlaced with the clothing of three other girls, and she ruffled through a few piles before finding shorts, a tank top, and Calvin Klein sandals, which she took into the bathroom and laid on the back of the toilet. Her nose still hadn't stopped bleeding, so she shoved toilet paper up both nostrils. She jumped into the shower, lathered herself, and rinsed. Then she did it again because she couldn't remember if she'd done it already.

As she got out of the shower and reached for the towel, she happened to catch a glimpse of herself in the mirror. Blood was running from both nostrils, soaking the toilet paper red, and going down over her mouth and breasts before dripping onto the floor in small uneven circles. She placed the towel over her nose and leaned back to slow the bleeding, but she was bleeding so much that she felt as if she were drinking the stuff. She leaned forward again. Pressure couldn't slow the blood anymore. A dam had broken, and she could do nothing but wait until all the liquid flowed out. She reached up to scratch her itchy ears, and her fingers came away wet with a reddish-black, syrupy fluid.

Carrie started to get dressed so she could go to the hospital when an intense pressure grew inside her stomach. The muscles convulsed violently, and before she could get a drink of water, hoping that would calm it, vomit erupted out of her mouth as though it had come from a fire hose. Because she kept her mouth closed, it sprayed through her teeth and came out her nose, choking her. It had the texture of oatmeal—a thick, black oatmeal, mostly liquid with mushy patches made of something she couldn't identify.

And the pain—it swept through her like an electric current. Every cell in her body had caught fire at the same time. But her head and her stomach were the worst. Her stomach was churning and growling, and every time she vomited, she felt as if the convulsions had torn a new hole in her stomach lining. And her head was pounding from a migraine that made her see stars. The light above her seemed harsh, and she flicked it off, then collapsed onto the bathroom floor in the dark.

Michelle Billings finished up at the pool and went to the bar set up outside to have one more shot of tequila. A cute guy she'd been flirting with all day had gotten her room number, and they were going to meet up later for some time out on the strip.

Of all the casinos, Michelle liked Caesar's Palace the best. She thought the way the old statues and the neon flashing lights came together was cool, like a weird nightmare. But they'd stayed at the Monte Carlo because someone's father was able to get them their room for free.

214

After sucking on a lime, she threw the rind into her empty shot glass and headed back to the hotel room she was sharing with three other girls. Sharing a queen was not exactly the ideal situation for her, but it was kind of fun. It reminded her of sleepovers she and her sister had when they were kids.

She walked into her room and shut the door behind her. "Hello?" No reply came, so she went in and collapsed onto the bed with a loud sigh. She closed her eyes and began to drift to sleep, but then she smelled something awful. The scent was like warm vomit that had been left out for days. She heard something from the bathroom.

"Hello? Heidi, is that you?"

She rose and walked over. The lights were off, and a streak of fear overcame her, giving her chills. Someone was on the floor. She flipped on the lights and screamed.

Carrie was lying on her back in a pool of blood that didn't seem real. The blood had spread across the bathroom tile like a wet rug and filled the corners. Congealed and curdling, it looked like gelatin.

Carrie quivered, and a stream of blood came out of her mouth and ran down her already-bloodstained neck. Only the whites of her eyes were showing, and she was trembling.

"Carrie!"

Her body convulsed so violently that she kicked her legs. They hit Michelle in the ankle and she slipped on the blood and fell forward on the sink. Black vomit spewed from Carrie's mouth, over Michelle's back.

Michelle pulled herself up using the sink and slipped in the putrid fluid, coating herself in it. Getting to her hands and knees, she crawled to the doorway and scrambled out of the room with an ear-piercing scream.

48

"Wait."

Samantha's heart beat against her ribs like a sledgehammer. She was still young enough that the actual concrete fear of death hadn't settled over her yet. She'd always been trying to prevent it in others or comforting those who had already lost people. She'd never had time to contemplate her own death. That one day, her life would be extinguished as easily as turning off a light had never entered her mind, until Robert Greyjoy was standing over her a month ago, telling her she was going to die. She had that same feeling again. Fate would flip a switch, and everything she was wouldn't exist anymore.

She had seen so much death in her life that it didn't seem tangible. She'd seen entire villages wiped off the face of the earth by a single virus that could barely be seen under the most powerful of microscopes. Samantha had watched hemorrhaging children suffer for weeks in hospital beds with open sores before dying, and it had never dawned on her that it could happen to her. She thought she was immune from it somehow because she was the one taking care of them.

She thought back to a young child in Nigeria who had lost both his parents to Ebola. He had watched them die and had still asked where they were days afterward. His mind had erased that memory because of the acute pain it caused. She wondered if any memories like that were floating around in her mind—things she repressed because she could not face the possibility that life could be nothing more than cruel, random chance.

And, with a gun pointed at her heart, she wondered if she had led the life that she truly wanted.

"Do you need a moment to prepare?" the man asked.

"Would you give it to me if I did?"

"Yes. I'm not a monster."

"Could've fooled me."

He grinned and lowered the gun. "People always ask me why I've chosen them. Why they're going to die. But you didn't ask. It's such a funny thing to see people expect good things in their life, that everything will turn out all right. We're parasites drifting through black space on top of a rock, and people are shocked when bad things happen to them. I think it would be more appropriate if people were shocked when good things happened to them."

"I wouldn't want to live that way—without hope."

"Hope was what was left in Pandora's box. Maybe people's lives aren't meant to have hope." He was silent a moment and then glanced back to Jane. "She's quite lovely, even like this. They gave her a sedative after I came in here and she saw the gun. I told them I was her husband. She called out for you."

Emotion tugged at her, and she swallowed, hoping to keep it down. "Leave her alone."

"I only take a life when I'm paid or when it amuses me. Taking the life of an unconscious convalescent wouldn't amuse me, and no one's paying me to do it."

"How much are they paying you to take my life?"

"They're not giving me money. In fact, when my employers get here, there won't be a use for money anymore."

"Who are your employers?"

"Unfortunately, you won't get to meet them, but they're coming. They'll be here soon, actually, once my work and the work of others like me across the world is finished."

"What is your work? Murdering doctors?"

"No. Eliminating resistance."

49

Howie woke in the dark, feeling only the intense heat. He couldn't hear anything but his own breathing. His eyelids fluttered, and they seemed sticky, as if they had been glued shut. Reaching up over his head, he touched smooth steel. When he forced himself up, pain shot into his shoulder with such intensity, he thought he might pass out. When his fingers found the space between his neck and shoulder, he felt the roughness of bandages.

He was in a box—a metal one that was about five feet by four feet. He thought of monkeys he'd seen on television that were crated and shipped off from Africa to the zoos or labs where they were destined to spend the rest of their lives. He felt like one of those monkeys now.

He guessed the slits in the box were for air, and he pressed his face against them to look out. He was inside what appeared to be a storage facility. At least a dozen other boxes were stacked around him, along with crates overflowing with supplies. A sliver of dim, golden light was coming through from the space underneath a door.

Howie sat back, trying to control the vertigo that was making his stomach feel like Jell-O. He was so hot that his eyes felt as though they were frying, and when he closed his lids, it was worse, like putting a blanket over them.

Weakness overtook him then, and he wanted nothing more than to lie down and die. Jessica was gone—probably taken back to a camp—and he could only pray that she was in a women's camp. His girlfriend was gone; so were his house, his cars, and his family. The only family he really had was his ex-wife's family. Her mother had been surprisingly gentle and loving with him, and Howie had grown close to her. But she passed from a heart attack at forty-nine years old. The cardiologist had told Howie that it was just one of those things they had no control over. Humans had no control over the most important things in life, really. He had felt so helpless then, so impotent. But that was nothing compared to how he felt in that box. Fate hadn't spun his life out of control; other men had—men from his own government, no less. They were meant to protect him.

He leaned back against the side of the box and thought he would close his eyes. No more running. No more fighting. He didn't have it in him.

He felt a warm sensation on his face. Sticky blood was coming out of his nose. He wiped at it softly but then stopped. What did it matter anyway?

He began to drift off to sleep, but laughter woke him, and he realized it was his own. He was about to die in a box. Despite all his wealth, the hundred or so employees who relied on him, the interviews with the media, and all the people who sought his advice as though he actually had something to teach… he was going to die alone in a box, like a sick dog.

He wondered where his father was now—a man in his sixties dating twenty-year-olds. Howie had an uncle somewhere, too, whom he hadn't seen in over a decade. The last time he'd seen him, his uncle was leaving on a world cruise and had asked Howie to come with him. He'd asked him not to be confined to one city, ever. Howie wanted to go so badly that he hadn't been able to sleep the night before his uncle was going to leave for his first stop: Florence. But he couldn't go. One face kept appearing to him every time he made up his mind to go and abandon everything. Jessica. But she was gone, and he was alone.

When Howie woke up the temperature was hotter than he remembered it being before. Sweat rolled off him as though he were in a sauna, and his clothes were drenched. His collar was also damp with blood. He started to peel his shirt off and then stopped. Death would probably come quicker if he allowed himself to dehydrate. He had no intention of dragging this out.

And then he heard something coming from another room, possibly next door, where the light was coming from, that made his heartbeat hammer in his ears—a piercing scream. He would have recognized that voice no matter where he was.

Jessica.

50

Duncan Adams waited for a long time outside the hospital. He spent most of that time walking around. He went across the street to a convenience store to get a drink. The cashier, who was reading a magazine, looked up.

"Hi."

"Hi," Duncan said.

"Just so you know, the credit card machine is down."

"I've got cash, thanks."

He went to the fridge, picked out a chocolate milk, and went to the cash register. He laid the cash on the counter. As the cashier counted out Duncan's change, he picked up the phone, put it to his ear, and then placed it back down.

"Can I ask you something?" the cashier asked. "Is your phone working?"

"No. No one's is."

He shook his head. "So weird."

Duncan went back to the hospital entrance and sat at the curb, drinking his milk. He checked his watch, and almost an hour had passed. He threw the empty bottle in a trash bin and went inside.

The hospital wasn't extremely busy, and two staff were talking about how bizarre it was that they hadn't seen any stabbings or shootings that night. But they had treated a lot of people with the flu. He told them that anyone with flu-like symptoms should be quarantined, and they stared at him as if he were a crazy person off the streets. He decided he had to find Sam. Maybe she could help convince them.

As he walked around a corner, he stepped around something on the floor, slowly realizing it was blood. Cautiously, he followed the small trail around a desk.

A nurse with a hole in her head was lying on top of a police officer. He bent down to check their pulses but then didn't. Their eyes already had the grayness of death. They had been gone for a while.

He stood up to go notify the staff, thinking they needed the police or more guardsmen at the hospital. Suddenly, another thought hit him, and he nearly lost his breath. *Sam.*

He ran to the elevator and took it to the quarantine floor. He dashed into Jane's room. The door hit someone and knocked them forward as Duncan saw the man standing next to the bed, with a pistol in his hand.

Without a thought, he ran at him.

The man fired the pistol, and the bullet grazed his shoulder as Duncan leapt on the man, who twisted him around and flung him into the wall. Duncan ran at him again, and at the last moment, he ducked and grabbed the man's legs, taking him down.

"Run, Sam!"

Samantha was screaming something, but he couldn't hear it because the man had slapped both his ears. The intense pain and the ringing told him that his eardrums had been ruptured. But he still had both hands on the man's firing arm. Samantha picked up a chair, ran over, and struck the stranger with it.

He reached up the arm to the pistol. The stranger was clearly too strong, and Duncan couldn't wrestle the pistol away. Instead, he stuck his finger over the trigger and fired. Four shots went off, four quiet spits that went into the ceiling. And the gun clicked empty.

The man punched him in the face and then savagely elbowed him multiple times. Duncan's grip loosened as Sam ran over with something else.

"Run, now!" he shouting at her as the man was getting to his feet. He wrapped both hands around Duncan's jaw, and the last thing he heard was Samantha's scream—and the crunch of his own spine.

Samantha screamed and ran out of the room, fear overtaking her. She was sobbing as she ran down the hall to the elevator and pushed the button. The stranger came out of the room and sprinted toward her. She kept pushing the button, refusing to acknowledge him, but she knew she wouldn't make it onto the elevator.

She backed up against the glass as he ran at her. He wasn't slowing down, and right before impact, she wrapped her arms around him and pushed back with her legs. His momentum went forward and hers went back, sending them crashing through the thin window.

A sensation of flying hit her, and she twisted to the side before they both slammed into the lawn from thirty feet up.

51

Howie shouted for his daughter but didn't get a response. She apparently couldn't hear anything else over her own screaming and crying.

He tried shaking the box, but nothing happened. The door on the outside was locked with a padlock that he could hear clink every time he pushed on the door. He pressed on the backside of the box. Leaning into it, he thrust back with his leg, and the metal gave a little. The box wasn't against the wall as he had originally thought.

Howie kicked again and again, and the metal caved a little each time. He kicked at least five more times before the corners of the box bent and gave way. After a final kick, the side was bent enough that he could push it off. It crashed to the floor, and he crawled out, his head spinning and the blood draining out of his nose.

He climbed off the counter the box was sitting on, then ran to the door where the screaming was coming from and opened it.

A guardsman, the only one in the room, was trying to tear Jessica's clothing off. Red handprints marked her face, and she was fighting as hard as she could. The guardsman heard the door open and turned as Howie sprinted at him.

The blow knocked the wind out of both of them, and Howie landed on top of him. Howie had his hands around the guard's throat, and some of his blood dripped into the other man's opened mouth and eyes. The guard screamed, trying to wipe away the blood.

Howie got a good grip on the man's throat, and his eyes bulged when Howie's grip tightened. He wasn't trying to get the blood off himself anymore, but, making hoarse, guttural sounds, he was scrambling to pull Howie's fingers away. Howie didn't let go, his arms straining like serpents wrapped around their next meal, until the man's body went limp beneath him.

He stood and turned to his daughter, who was crying and holding torn clothing to her body. Holding his head away, he put his arms around her, and she cried for a long time. He wasn't sure how long because he was drifting in and out of consciousness.

"We need to go," he said.

He took the guard's rifle, which was propped against the wall, and put the strap around himself as they opened another door that led to a dark hallway. He walked slowly to make as little noise as possible but couldn't hear anyone else. As they rounded a corner, he heard laughter coming from another room.

He motioned for Jessica to wait in the hall and then glanced in. Four guardsmen playing poker were drinking and laughing, their rifles stacked neatly on a table across the room. He lifted the strap of the rifle off himself and walked calmly into the room, pointing the barrel at the first guardsman's head.

"I want the keys to any jeeps outside."

They sat silently, glancing at each other, until a blond one with a cigar in his mouth took the cigar out and said, "Fuck you. You want—"

The round tore into the side of his head and burst his brains over the table, staining the playing cards red. The body fell to the side into one of the others. The remaining guards didn't move.

"I don't have time. The keys, now, or I'll kill all of you and find them myself."

After the men were locked away in boxes in the room he had woken up in, Howie and Jessica exited through a side door. The building was just a warehouse. Out front were two jeeps and a Humvee. He unlocked the passenger door to the Humvee and helped Jessica inside. He got into the driver's seat, started it, and pulled away.

52

Samantha felt broken. Her hip was twisted, and her knee burned. She tried to lift herself, but the pain in her legs and hip was too much. She managed to roll onto her back. Next to her, the stranger was unconscious.

She rolled to the other side, and a pain unlike anything she had ever felt before pierced her ribs. It took her breath away, and she groaned as she forced herself up. Limping, she made her way to the hospital entrance.

She went to the all-night pharmacy and walked behind the counter. A young pharmacist with glasses and acne was the only employee, left to fill prescriptions and work the register. He yelled at her, threatening to call the police.

"Go ahead," she rasped.

Going through the shelves, she found some Percocet and took two of them without water. The young pharmacist stared at her in disbelief.

Sam hobbled out and took the elevators to the third floor. She went to Jane's room, where Duncan was lying on the floor, limp, his eyes open to the ceiling. The guards weren't there, and she wondered what had happened to them and if the man had killed them, too.

She bent down, weeping softly, and felt for a pulse. She couldn't feel one.

She closed his eyes and kissed his lips, which were already cold. She rose and looked at her sister. Lifting the canopy, she pulled at the bed. Her hips and ribs were in agony, but she didn't stop—not until she had pushed the hospital bed away from the wall. Then she got behind it and pushed it out of the room.

Slowly, with pain pulsating at her with every step, she took the elevators to the top floor and wheeled her sister into the room with the old woman at the end of the hall. She closed the door behind her, then hobbled downstairs. Outside, where she had been lying a few minutes ago, the stranger was gone.

Staggering through the parking lot, she went up the street to wait at an intersection for the light to turn. Her knee felt torn to pieces, and she couldn't put hardly any weight to it. Crossing the street, she noticed several choppers above her and that few cars filled the street.

Samantha stepped out into the road and waited for the first car to come by.

Howie drove through town, constantly checking his daughter, who was staring absently at the passing city. He thought a long time about what to say to her, about how to describe what that man was trying to do and why. But no explanation he could give would be adequate. When they could get away with it, all men were capable of evil.

"Are you thirsty?"

"No," she whispered.

Howie kept his eyes on her for a long time. She resembled her mother more and more, and it made him miss her. It made him regret his arrogance and stupidity for thinking he could ignore her, cheat on her, and still have her stick around.

When he turned his eyes back to the road, he had to slam on the brakes and swerve. The Humvee's tires squealed as it skidded to the curb and the front tires ran up onto the sidewalk.

He turned to peer out the rear window. The woman who had been standing in the road was limping toward them. She was injured, and a cut on her head was bleeding.

"Please," she said. "I need help. I'm not infected."

He hesitated a few seconds and was about to put it in drive, but Jessica gave him a look. She was watching intently what he was about to do. The fact was, he didn't know how much longer he was going to be around. What memories of himself he left her with was suddenly very important to him.

Howie stepped out of the Humvee and helped the woman in before shutting the door and pulling away. As he drove past a hospital, Howie saw a man in a disheveled suit standing in the parking lot, searching for something. They exchanged glances before Howie turned his attention back to the road.

"What happened to you?" he asked.

"You have to get me to a medical facility," she rasped.

"There was a hospital back there."

"No." She shook her head gently as her eyes closed and then opened. "There's a military facility."

"Lady, we are not going anywhere near a medical facility. But I'd be happy to drop you off somewhere if you need."

"I have to get help and come back. My sister needs my help still."

As he turned to get on the interstate, Howie saw, to his horror, that a roadblock had been set up. He was about to do a U-turn, hoping they didn't push it, when one of the guardsmen stepped forward and held up his hand, indicating for the Humvee to stop.

Howie reached for the rifle that he had placed in the backseat.

"No," the woman said. "Let me talk."

The guardsman came to the window and peered in. He was turning away to shout to his fellow soldiers when the woman spoke up. "My name is Dr. Samantha Bower. I'm here at the request of General Clyde Olsen. I need his assistance. Please call him for me."

The guardsman was silent and then spoke into a device on his shoulder. "Get Lieutenant General Olsen on the horn, Kelly."

53

Ian came to and lifted himself off the grass. Samantha was gone. Disoriented, he stood. His vision was fuzzy, and all the general shapes before him appeared to have an aura. Beginning at his toes, he stretched or flexed every part of his body.

His leg was fractured at the fibula. Several ribs were cracked, and he likely had a compound fracture at T6 and T7 in his spinal column. His acromion was splintered, probably broken into several pieces, and numerous metacarpals were broken, as well. Acute pain shocked him with every movement of his body, and his left arm and leg were numb, but his left foot was tingling with hot needles.

He walked over the grass, ignoring the intense pain that was commanding him to lie down and be still.

He had forgotten where he had told Katherine to wait for him in the vast parking lot. As he stood thinking about where to go, long strands of drool dropped from his mouth, and he wiped them with the back of his sleeve.

He had let anger take control of him, and this was the result. He could have calmly taken Samantha Bower into his arms and crushed her throat like melon. Instead, his rage emptied out of him, and he had dashed at her in a full sprint, oblivious to the window behind her. He would do better next time.

Remembering that he had asked Katherine to stay at the front entrance, he shuffled his way there. She was gone.

"Stupid girl."

He scanned the area around him and saw a Humvee drive by. The driver wasn't military, and Ian hoped he would stop, but he didn't. Someone ducked in the backseat.

The Humvee turned a corner and was gone.

Ian felt lightheaded, and before he could control himself, he blacked out again.

He rose sometime later; he wasn't sure how much later. His head pounded from what he guessed was a severe concussion, and he had to lean against a tree in the parking lot until the world stopped spinning. He remembered a Humvee driving by before he blacked out.

As he was about to go into the road to find another car, he saw movement out of the corner of his eye. Turning toward it, he spotted Katherine standing at the back of the car, staring at something in the trunk. He limped toward her. She had moved his briefcase back there and opened it.

"Tell me that's not what I think it is," she said.

He was quiet, unable to muster the strength to speak. "It is," he said softly.

"Even you can't be this much of a monster."

Holding her gaze, he pressed something on the device and then reached up and closed the trunk. "I am."

He noticed himself in the reflection of the back window. He was covered in blood, and his arm was bent at an awkward angle. He was leaning to the side as if his back couldn't support his weight, and he'd gone from a handsome young man to someone who appeared to have risen from an awful grave.

"What happened to you?"

"You need to drive me to the airport."

"I'll pull out."

She got into the car, turned it on, and backed out of the parking spot. She turned the wheel at an angle so that Ian could climb in and then stopped. He hobbled over.

She twisted the wheel hard to the right, slanting the car toward Ian, and slammed the pedal down. The tires squealed, making smoke, as the car rocketed forward. Making impact with Ian sounded more like something falling on top of her car rather than hitting it at the front.

Ian flew and slammed to the ground, then rolled at least ten feet. She swallowed, her mouth dry and her mind blank. She hit the accelerator again, and the car jumped up, then fell as if she'd driven over a speed bump.

She sat in the car, staring at the unmoving body before slowly getting out. Ian was on his back, spitting up blood. Tire marks burned his chest, and his hands were black and lay useless by his side.

Steadily, she walked up to him. His face should have been filled with terror, but he looked... serene.

He grinned at her. "It's too late," he gasped.

She watched him, confused, when she heard something—a ticking, but not quite. It was more of an electronic beep every few seconds. She started to run in the opposite direction.

The explosion was so massive and blinding that she didn't even have time to realize she was dying.

54

Samantha wouldn't have even noticed the explosion if not for Clyde Olsen sitting across from her on the plane.

"What the hell is that?" He pointed out the window.

From the plane, the detonation appeared only to the passengers sitting next to the window, who had happened to glance outside at the moment of the flash.

A tube of light, almost thirty meters tall, was followed by an explosion that could've taken out a soccer field. Like a black hole, the explosion sucked in light, and then after another, smaller explosion, a thin mist descended over the city.

She turned her head. Seated across from her were the man and his young daughter whom she had convinced General Olsen to bring along as they fled the state. They had saved her life, and Samantha was obligated to save theirs.

All of this occurred amidst utter calm and quiet. Neighborhood by neighborhood, the military had rounded up the citizens of Los Angeles and put them into camps. The ones with pull—relatives of federal employees, for example—were taken to the nicer hotels and allowed to stay there of their own recognizance. Everyone else, rich or poor, was stuck in a cage. But the guards were taking bribes to let people go.

Stretched to the brink across Southern California and then Northern, the National Guard didn't have enough men to police itself. And most of the local law enforcement had been rounded up along with the civilians. Only the ones on duty, who were easily recognizable, had been given a place next to their captors.

In some places, Olsen had told her, guards were apparently letting people out for as little as a thousand dollars cash, jewelry, guns, or cars—anything the guards could get their hands on. The only people truly stuck in the cages were the poor and middle class who couldn't pay up.

The operation had been a disaster from the get-go. The military only later recognized the contingencies they hadn't planned for. They had probably thought it would be a simple operation, and that all they had to do was ensure no one left the state. They hadn't anticipated the bribery or the failing infrastructure. After one day, water and electricity was dwindling in most of the state, including the military bases.

But the mist that had settled over the city after the explosion was something else that no one had ever seen or could have planned for.

Olsen's cell phone buzzed as they flew over the California-Nevada border.

"Olsen… yes… yes… What other cities? Okay. Okay. Roger that."

He hung up and stared out the window at the gray dawn, twirling the phone in his fingers before it dropped and hit the metal floor with a ding.

"What's wrong?" Samantha asked, the pain medication causing her speech to slur and slow.

"Three other explosions. Nashville, Manhattan, and DC."

"What are they?"

"I don't know. But they're all reporting the same thing. A green mist."

A single horrifying thought gripped her mind. It sent shivers up her back, and though she was numb from the medication, she knew that something had happened that would change the course of society. As soon as the thought was articulated with words, she knew it to be true.

The mist was Agent X.

From the way Olsen was acting, Samantha knew that the military hadn't had any idea that was going to occur. Life was truly unpredictable, a string of random events interspersed with fleeting glimpses of reason and order. But that was illusory. In the end, the events tying a life together were dictated more by circumstance than people believed. So many unknown variables existed, so many forces pulling in each direction, that it seemed funny to her that she had ever thought order endured along with the anarchy. She was almost embarrassed that she had been so naïve.

The young girl was asleep, but she stirred and cuddled up to her father. He gently pushed her away and then leaned against the window. He was pale and sweating, and he had gone to the bathroom twice on the plane.

He noticed her watching him. Glancing at his daughter, he stood up and walked past Olsen. When he came close to Samantha, he said, "Can I talk to you, Doctor?"

Samantha rose, leaning on the seats for support, and followed him. They stood far enough away that General Olsen couldn't hear.

"You're with the Centers for Disease Control, right?"

"Yes."

"You're a virus doctor?"

"In a sense, yes."

"What is this thing?"

"It's something like a variant of the poxvirus called black pox. But it's mutated a few times, so we called it Agent X. An intern called it that, and it stuck because we didn't know what else to call it."

"It should be called Red Pox. It seems like all it does is make you bleed."

She nodded. "You know you're infected, don't you?"

He glanced at his daughter. "Is there a cure?"

"We don't even have a cure for the common cold or flu. There are no cures for a virus. You can slow them down or prevent them, but once you have them, they have to run their course."

"So there's nothing?"

"There's an experimental drug that was being developed by a laboratory in Nigeria that I was working with. It's a type of drug that can identify infected cells and then destroy those cells, essentially halting replication of a virus. It might work with something like this. But the research was taken over by the government and then buried. There's nothing else I can think of."

"Is there any way"—he paused to cough—"someone like me could get it. Or maybe someone like you?"

"No. We'd have to fly to Nigeria first and then see how far they got with it. I don't think it ever got approved for human trials. By the time we got there and it was ready…"

"I'd be dead." He took a deep breath. "I don't even know your name."

"Samantha Bower."

"Samantha, my name is Harold Burke. I know we're strangers, and I never thought I would ask this of anyone, much less someone I don't know, but my daughter is the only thing in the world I have left. If you could… until you find her mother, I mean… I don't have anybody left that would…"

He said it so genuinely, filled with so much utter humiliation and so much hope that she would accept, that it tore out her heart. She thought of her own mother and the nights she'd spent crying when her father had passed away, bargaining with God that she would do anything if her husband could come back to them. She had three children to look after by herself, and her mother worked two jobs to provide for them. She gave up everything in her life so her children could have a chance at a better one. Children were everyone's weakness.

"I'll take care of her."

He nodded, tears in his eyes. "Thank you."

After a moment, he coughed again and then made room so she could get by without having to get near him. Samantha was all the way to her seat when the plane's side door opened. The vacuum instantly sucked out anything that wasn't screwed or strapped down, and deafening high-pitched squealing of dropping pressure filled the plane. It flung her off balance, and Olsen had to grab her to keep her in place. Her ears popped, and a terrible sucking sound filled the cabin as things bounced off the metal interior.

By the time she saw what had happened, one of Olsen's soldiers had grabbed the door and pulled it closed. But Harold Burke wasn't there. He was already flying through the air to his death.

Kansas City, Kansas

Mark Sheffield walked out of his office to get some fresh air. He'd had a cough and a fever all morning, but his boss, a prick named Ted, had refused to allow him to take a sick day. They had a meeting that afternoon with an investor in their marketing and SEO company, and Mark was the salesman. He went to the meeting and made it through only by stopping to cough about five times. After the last bout, he glanced down and saw that his handkerchief was coated with blood.

Outside the building, he leaned against a tree planted near the sidewalk. The sound of cars whizzing by annoyed him. Someone was running a trimmer along the grass, and the buzz-saw racket was grinding against Mark's nerves. He would have yelled at the guy, even thrown something at him, but he didn't have the strength. He had enough energy to know to go to the hospital, and that was it. He texted his wife to come pick him up and then didn't move from the spot.

Ted texted several times, asking Mark where the hell he was and saying that he needed to come to an early dinner to schmooze the clients. *Going home to sleep,* he replied.

When his wife arrived, Mark climbed into the car and put on his seat belt. She stared at him without driving.

"What's wrong?" he asked.

"You look like crap."

"Thanks. Just take me to a hospital, will ya?"

"Mark, you look terrible. What's going on?"

"How the fuck do I know?"

On the way to the hospital, he started vomiting—little globs of blood at first. Then torrents of the stuff came out in long streams and soaked the floor mats. His wife was frantically shouting into her phone at someone, but the pain was so intense that he couldn't hear her. He couldn't hear anything, and soon, he couldn't see either. And he understood, from the amount of the warm fluid that was coming out of him, that his eyes and ears were bleeding.

Before he bled out, he heard his wife screaming in his ear that she couldn't live without him. He wanted to say, "Yes you can." But no words came.

Miami, Florida

Jennifer Mills finished her beer and then played absently with her nachos while she looked over her balcony at the people below. All the chips were still on the plate. She had put one chip into her mouth and then spit it back out because even the thought of food was so disgusting that she might have to run to the bathroom and hurl. Instead, she drank ice water, which even alone made her queasy.

Masood, her boyfriend, came out of the bathroom naked, smiling at her. She wanted to protest and tell him that she wasn't in the mood anymore, but getting it over with seemed easier. They kissed on the balcony, and he took her hand and forced her to play with him as he lifted her and took her to her bed. He pulled down her skirt and then entered her.

She didn't feel pleasure or pain. She was numb. Her stomach was bloated even though she hadn't eaten anything since the day before. Small pimply sacs had appeared on her skin, but Masood either didn't care or didn't notice. He was grunting and thrusting inside her as though it were the last time he would ever be with a woman again.

He bent down, put his mouth over hers and his tongue down her throat, and before she even knew what was happening, she spewed into his mouth. He had sealed his lips so tightly around hers that the vomit shot right over his tongue, and he swallowed a lot of it.

He jumped off and spit blood over the room as she kept saying, "I'm sorry, I'm sorry." She noticed that his genitals were covered in blood, and when he saw that, he ran into the bathroom, shouting profanity at her about not telling him she was on her period.

She was too weak to respond that she'd had her period the previous week. So instead, she lay back and listened to the water running in the shower as she dozed off.

Kyoto, Japan

Aiki Ito screamed as the doctors told her to push. The baby—a boy—was going to be huge, they said. His father had been large when he was born, too. This pregnancy had been a difficult one, and for the past three days Ito had been so sick that she couldn't get out of bed. She was going to get this baby out of her, no matter what.

The pain was intense and ran up into her guts, chest, and neck. Even with an epidural, every little needle prick felt like an event that lasted forever. Her skin was extremely sensitive, and she could only keep her eyes open for so long at one time because the pain made her faint. The lights of the hospital room seemed harsh and caused her retinas to ache.

The doctor was yelling at her to push, and she did. The doctor pulled the baby out, and Ito cried when she saw him. She focused on the baby for so long that she didn't notice the frantic movements of the doctor and nurses. They were running around, shouting to each other. Something was wrong. The bleeding wouldn't stop.

"We're doing everything we can," the doctor kept telling her, in an effort to calm her down, but the bleeding wouldn't stop.

And then she felt something so mind-numbingly painful that she thought it would kill her. Something inside seemed to detach from everything else, as though a piece of her had come off. The pressure made its way down, almost like a lump heading for the drain in a bathtub. As she reached down to touch where the pain was, the lump slipped out of her, and the nurses screamed.

Her organs were coming out with rivers of blood.

55

General Kirk Lancaster was in Maine when he found out about the detonation. Even during a time of emergency, the one place he didn't want to be was at the Pentagon. When he was there, he was checking his phone and his e-mail every minute or two and driving himself insane. So instead, he turned off his phone and drove to his family's cabin in Eastport. He would eventually call up his wife and three boys, but right then, he needed the solitude, more than he had thought he did.

He was sitting in his small fishing boat with the hook in the water, a beer in his hand, and the sun on his face, when he decided he should probably turn on his phone. He had thirteen unheard messages and even more e-mails—fifty-six. He flipped through some, purely out of curiosity, as his underlings should have been able to cover everything for at least an afternoon.

He saw the subject line in one e-mail, and his heart dropped. He immediately called Martin.

"Where were you?" Martin asked.

"I thought you quit?"

"I'm temporarily back. I called all around for you."

"That's not important. What the fuck happened?"

"As to the why or how, I don't have a clue. Clearly an attack within our borders."

"What do you have?"

"I got witnesses in all four cities. Same thing everywhere. A man and a suitcase and an explosion. Except for LA. The witness there was a nurse working at a hospital. She saw a man lying injured on the ground in their parking lot, and a woman ran away from him. And that's when the blast occurred."

"Did any of them survive?"

"No. But it looks like this explosion wasn't the primary function of the device. The explosion's diameter was only about twenty feet. The primary function appears to be the release of the mists."

Lancaster stayed silent on the phone for a long time. "You're not telling me—"

"I don't know yet, sir. We're having the mist properly tested to see for sure. But preliminary assessments are coming back positive for a type of poxvirus."

Lancaster put his hand over his forehead and bent down. He felt ill. "Holy shit, Martin. Holy shit…"

"Sir, do we have any ideas as to who could have done this?"

"Four chemical weapons simultaneously detonated in the four largest cities? No, Martin. I don't have a fucking clue who could have done this. I'm guessing it's not some cave-dwellers in Pakistan. But whoever they are, we better hope they're not planning something else, 'cause we were just brought to our fucking knees."

56

Hank Kraski sat on the bench at the park, watching the pigeons as they flew down. An old man was feeding them stale bread. Hank counted over fifty pigeons and was delighted to watch them flap around and wrestle and peck at each other for dominance.

Before too long, a woman with curly red hair and a black suit came and sat next to him. They were there early in the morning, and in the light of dawn, she looked stunning. Something had been there between them long ago but was gone now.

"Ian's dead," she said.

"I know."

"You trained Greyjoy, and he trained Ian. You guys are becoming an extinct species."

"We were always meant to be."

"All four detonations went off perfectly. We had three more in Europe and two in Asia last night. We didn't feel that Australia and Africa were warranted, and unless you wanted to take out penguins, Antarctica should be obvious."

"I agree."

She checked her watch. "I don't know if they briefed you on this, but a certain percentage of the population has a natural immunity to black pox."

"What percentage?"

"Point oh-oh-oh one. About seven thousand people on the earth will be completely immune to its effects, and it's genetic, as well. A dominant gene from what we can tell. It should display in their children, which should push that number up but probably to no more than twenty thousand."

He nodded. "We're anticipating ninety-five percent population loss. We can handle another twenty thousand people on top of the survivors."

She paused. "I couldn't sleep last night. Do you realize what we've done? What we've all done, Hank? We've changed the course of human history. It was going one way, and we came along, and it will follow a divergent path now."

He watched the pigeons. "How do you know this wasn't the path it was supposed to follow?"

Turning to look at her, he felt those old feelings resurface. He couldn't remember why he hadn't acted on them when he'd had the chance. Work, maybe. But the memory was so dusty with time, he couldn't think of a single good reason why they hadn't spent their lives together.

Her face was perfect—perfect and simple—even without makeup, which he found most people put on too much of anyway. She had been a model in the '80s, if he remembered correctly. His predecessor had seen her on some runway in Spain and had decided they needed to have her. His predecessor. *How odd to say that.* He figured every generation would soon have predecessors and be looking back, wondering how the hell they had become the ones in charge.

"If this doesn't work," she said, "if we're betrayed… then we just killed our own species."

Hank shrugged. "We would eventually die out anyway. Intelligence is counter-evolutionary. The species becomes wise enough to invent more and more efficient methods to kill itself. We were in a very long process of self-destruction."

She swallowed. "I didn't think the morning would look so pretty. I thought it would be overcast or raining, something."

He grinned. "Death on this scale probably has a tendency to surprise everyone."

57

Rick Bolton wrapped his tent and rolled the sleeping bag tightly. Early-morning Yosemite always had a certain vibe to it, especially far away from any cabins and parking lots. Something in the pine-scented air or the way the breeze whistled through the trees brought him a sense of calm that he really needed.

He'd been there a lot as a kid and remembered the murders that had taken place. A mother and her fifteen-year-old daughter, an exchange student, and another young woman who worked for Yosemite had been killed. The decapitated body of the fourth victim had led police to Cary Stayner, who was later convicted of all four murders.

The number of visitors to Yosemite had declined when word got out about the Yosemite Killer. When the brutal sexual assault and torture details came out, camping in Yosemite became almost non-existent. Rick still went. His father had said they'd caught the killer, and he had only targeted females, so he and Rick were fine.

Rick was excited he and his father would have the entire park to themselves one summer when he was ten, but he hadn't enjoyed it much. A darkness, something heavy that seemed to stick to the skin, hung over everything when they were there. Two days into a six-day trip, his father packed up and said it was time to go.

Rick looked over at the final tent and saw the feet of his son and daughter sticking out. His thirteen-year-old son, Marcus, was snoring so loudly that Rick was amazed his daughter, Trudy, could sleep. He peeked in through the lip in the tent. Sure enough, they were both passed out. Taking out a water bottle, he spilled a few drops on each of their foreheads, and they groaned and stirred.

"What time is it?" Marcus asked.

"Seven o'clock," Rick said, then took a sip of the water before replacing the lid.

The six-day trip seemed to fly by. His work as a professor of anthropology routinely took him out of the state or country for long research projects and sabbaticals, and he tried to take his children with him whenever he could. Since their mother's passing two years before, he was all they had.

His boy sat up and rubbed the sleep out of his eyes. "Did you get what we came for?"

"Sure did," Rick replied, taking a small plastic container from his backpack. Wrapped up in cellophane were several arrowheads. "Anasazi. They weren't believed to be up this far north. They're mostly found in New Mexico. This is definitely their handiwork, though. It'll be an exciting paper."

Marcus swirled his finger in the air and said, "Yay."

Rick smacked him playfully, and Marcus tried to tackle him. Rick lifted him off his feet and got him onto his back. He pinned him, then held him there while one of his hands went down to his armpit and tickled.

"Eight years of wrestling, boy. You can't take your old man yet."

Marcus was laughing. "Stop, stop! I'm gonna piss myself."

Rick stopped and got off him. He helped the boy up, then smacked his bottom and told him to pack up the tent and his gear.

Trudy got up and went over to the edge of the trees to brush her teeth. When she was done, she got on her phone and mumbled something under her breath when she couldn't get reception.

"You know, there are other things to look at than a phone screen."

"I know. I'm waiting for a text from Alexis 'cause Brian asked her to that dance I was telling you about, and I wanna see if she said yes."

He shook his head. "You're eleven. You know what I was doing at eleven? I was outside, digging stuff up to see if I could find anything cool."

"Good for you, Dad. But you guys didn't have iPhones."

He grinned and helped Marcus finish packing.

When they were done, they headed out of the national park in their RV. Soon, they were on the I-5, going south, back to their home in Westwood in the heart of Los Angeles.

Marcus watched movies on his tablet, and Trudy played games on her phone. Rick frequently glanced back at them and smiled to himself. But occasionally, a pain would tug at his belly, and he would feel sullen and heavy, as though his thoughts and movements were working their way through water.

Trudy looked like her mother.

The drive wasn't that bad. But along the way were abandoned jeeps and roadblocks with no one tending to them. An uneasiness came over him, but he didn't know what else to do other than drive.

When he finally admitted to himself that no other cars were on the freeway, as if it had been abandoned, his uneasiness turned to panic.

"Either of you getting reception yet?"

"Not me," Marcus said.

"Me neither."

They were back in Los Angeles in five hours. In fact, he had never made the drive in that amount of time.

He parked at a truck stop outside the city and stretched his neck. Trudy was dozing on the bed in the back. He kissed her, then headed outside to the bathroom; hoping to find some other people that could tell him what the hell was going on. He wondered if the freeways had been closed because of some terrorist attack or natural disaster and they just hadn't gotten the message.

As he stepped outside, he noticed two empty cars in the lot. Rick went to the restroom and pissed at one of the urinals, yawning and stretching his shoulder, which had been injured in a college wrestling bout and never been quite the same.

When he finished and turned toward the sink, he saw something on the wall. Dark and dry, a smear led down into the stall. Spread over an enormous portion of the wall, it looked like blood.

From where he was standing, Rick couldn't see in. He walked over slowly. "Hello? Is someone there?" No reply. He crouched lower for some reason and felt stupid for doing so. So he stood up, went right over, and pushed the stall door open with his boot.

Inside, a man was huddled over a toilet. He was wearing a suit and fancy Italian leather shoes. His head was hanging over like a wet rag, and the entire stall was caked in dried blood. The walls, the floor, even the ceiling had been spattered.

"Um, hello? Do you want me to call an ambulance?"

Rick glanced to the door of the bathroom and then back to the man. He wondered if he should try to call the police or check on him first. But what did it matter if he was alive or dead? He would call the police, just the same.

He swallowed and took a step forward. Approaching the man from behind, he reached down to grab his hips and flip him over.

The man let out a gurgled, horrifying scream and spun onto his back. Rick jumped, and the man reached for him as more blood shot out of his mouth. But it barely looked like blood.

The man was covered in sores or chicken pox. But Rick had seen chicken pox when Trudy had them, and that wasn't chicken pox. The man's skin was bumpy, but it appeared to have been burnt. Some of it was falling off.

Rick ran out of the bathroom to get his phone and call the police. Then he heard his daughter scream.

58

Samantha's plane landed at Dobbins Air Force Base, and she waited until it had come to a complete stop before unbuckling herself. She glanced at Jessica. The young girl was sitting in shock, staring out the window. She had asked where her father was twice, and no one told her.

As they stepped off the plane, Sam put her arm around the girl's shoulders and shuttled her over to an awaiting jeep. They rode in silence, but Jessica didn't remove Samantha's arm. In fact, she placed her head on Sam's ribs, and Sam kept her arm over her, as if she could shield her from what they both knew was coming.

When the jeep stopped in front of Samantha's home, she debated for an instant. Olsen had given orders for the child to be taken into protective custody. But she knew what that meant—a night at a military base and then into state care. That wasn't what Sam had promised Harold.

Without so much as a peep from the driver, Samantha helped the young girl out of the jeep, and they walked inside the house. The house was immaculately clean.

Sam checked her watch, and it read 9:00 a.m. The nurse usually came at around ten. The maids came twice a week, and a physical therapist was over twice a week to take her mother out for walks and to exercise on the equipment in the basement.

"There's a spare room over there," Samantha said. "You have your own bathroom. We'll go tomorrow and try and find you some new clothes."

"Where's my dad?" she asked.

Samantha locked eyes with her. The girl's light-blue eyes were full of confusion and fury. She already knew where her father was; she had known it the moment she'd woken on the plane to the awful suction of an open door and didn't see him there. But Sam guessed she needed to hear it.

"Your father is gone, Jessica. I'm sorry. He passed away to save the rest of us."

She nodded, glancing down at the floor. "What about my mom?"

"I don't know. There's no communication in or out of California, so I don't know what's happened to your mom. But we'll look for her today, okay?"

She turned without saying anything and went into the room Sam had pointed to. Sam waited a few moments and then poked her head in. Jessica was on the futon, curled up in a ball, and staring out the window at the sunlight that was flooding the street. Sam wondered what she could say to make it better, to ease her loss. But she couldn't come up with anything. Jessica hadn't just lost her father. Everything she had ever known was gone, and she would never get it back.

None of them would.

Samantha collapsed on the couch in the front room, her face in her hands, and cried. When she finished, no tears were left. She thought of Duncan and the sweet way he would text her with funny photos to make her laugh.

She was grieving, though she didn't recognize it as such. He would have asked her to marry him soon. Neither one of them had had any doubt about that. It was only a matter of finding the perfect moment. But it had never come. Instead, she was left with memories and a cold, empty feeling that the way her life was supposed to turn out had not materialized. Though she wanted to believe that, to revel in her grief, a part of her told her she would have said no, and it made her feel guilty. At least, she thought, Jane and her family had made it out.

"Are you okay?" Jessica was standing there.

Sam wiped the tears away and said, "Yeah."

"I don't think I can sleep."

Sam patted the cushion on her couch, and Jessica walked over and sat down as Sam put her shirt to her face and cleaned off the salty tears. She wrapped her arm around Jessica, and they leaned back on the couch. Before they had a chance to say anything to each other, both of them were asleep.

60

Rick burst through the bathroom door and saw a man banging on his RV.

"Hey!" Rick ran over, grabbed him by the shoulders, and flung him away. He went in for a kick as the man was still struggling to get up and stopped.

The man was pale, and his eyes were rimmed so red that they looked painted. His clothes were stained black and wet, and Rick immediately knew it was blood. He jumped back as the man vomited so violently one of his eyes popped out of the socket. The slick, wet cord allowed it to dangle over the pavement as the vomit continued to flow.

Rick ran to the RV and tried to open the door, but it was locked. He banged on it and called out to Trudy. Marcus opened the door, and Rick jumped in, then shut the door behind him before locking it again. He ran up to the front to look out the windshield.

The day was warm and quiet, and with senses newly attuned from fear, he heard everything he had missed before. Or, in this case, he noticed what he hadn't heard.

No airplanes in the sky. No cars on the interstate. No voices outside. He turned on the radio and got static on every station. Rick pulled out his phone and dialed 9-1-1, but got a busy tone. He tried Googling the nearest police precinct, but the Internet on his phone wasn't working.

"Is your internet working, Trudy?"

"No, it hasn't worked for three days. I thought it was the canyons."

Rick sat in the driver's seat for a moment, staring out at the truck stop, thinking about the man with the face that appeared to be falling off. His flesh had been ragged, as though it were weak from being soaked in water and were slipping off his skull.

Rick started the RV and headed back onto the interstate. Trudy was sitting up in the passenger seat, and Marcus was on the floor behind him.

"What's happening, Daddy?" Trudy asked.

"I don't know."

They passed several cars, but none of them were moving. They were all pulled over to the side of the road without occupants. As they rolled into Los Angeles, a heavy, dark, feeling came over Rick, and for some reason, it was familiar. But he couldn't place it for a long time, until they saw a body in the middle of the road.

A man, maybe in his mid-twenties, was flat on his back, and some birds were picking at his belly, which was exposed underneath a dirty tank top. His face was bloody and torn up, and all his limbs were a dark black, as though they had been barbequed.

Rick stopped behind the corpse, recognizing the feeling he'd had before. In Yosemite, when they had entered the place where the Yosemite Killer had spread terror and evil for months, he'd felt the same.

"Dad?" Marcus said.

"Yeah."

"You gonna go around him?"

"Yeah," Rick said, not realizing he had been stopped for a long time. He rolled the RV around and continued down the interstate.

"Look at that," Marcus said.

Corpses were piled on the side of the road. A massive accident had occurred. At least twenty to thirty cars were strewn about like children's toys, rolled over or thrown onto the surrounding fields.

Bodies were everywhere. But the bodies didn't appear to have been flung around by the accident. These bodies had collapsed from something else. And the road was painted a faded red, with droplets thrown around like on a canvas painted by a drunken artist. It was so out of the ordinary that Rick's mind couldn't recognize the red paint for what it was: gallons of blood from the body of every person who had died out here.

"I'm scared, Daddy."

"We're safe in here," he said, unable to sound convincing. He caught her eyes, trying to appear as upbeat and positive as possible. "We're safe in here, sweetheart. Go lay down on the bed. We'll be home soon."

He pulled the RV over the median and around the corpses. Then he continued down the interstate, but what they saw was no different. Corpses rotted in the sun while birds, coyotes, and dogs tore at them. He kept driving, following the speed limit, and then grasping how pointless that seemed, he sped up to seventy-five and barreled toward his home as if that were their safe house and none of this would be real if they could get there.

The inner city was even worse. Bodies lay in the gutter like trash, and cars had run through convenience stores, wrapped around light poles, and flipped upside down. He didn't see anyone out.

Rick's home was up on a hill overlooking the city. To get there he had to go through Laurel Canyon, and he rolled down his windows so he could smell the eucalyptus leaves. The wind hit his face and made him feel better. He glanced in his rearview, and both his children were sitting attentively on the bed, neither of them speaking. Their eyes were glued to the windows, and he knew they were scanning for more dead bodies.

Pulling into their driveway, he stopped and put on the parking brake. None of them moved. Rick turned to them, and they exchanged glances.

"Why don't you guys stay here a minute," he said. "Just while I check out the house."

He walked outside and shut the door behind him. The bright sun was hot on his face, and he scanned his home, a five-bedroom built right on a cliff over the canyon, then walked to it.

61

Samantha woke to the sound of ringing. She checked her cell phone, but the batteries were long dead, and she realized her home phone was ringing.

Jessica was still asleep, her head nestled comfortably underneath Sam's arm. Samantha calmly lifted her arm and rose from the couch. She didn't know what time it was, but bright sunshine was coming through all the windows. A note from her mother's nurse was on the coffee table, letting her know that her mother had been fed and changed and that she hadn't wanted to wake Sam. It also asked who the girl was and said that she was adorable.

Samantha walked to the phone in the kitchen and answered it. "This is Samantha."

"Samantha, I didn't know if you'd made it back. This is Freddy."

Her boss—he was the person in the entire world she least wanted to talk to. "What do you need, Freddy?"

"Um, well, I don't know what to say. I heard about Duncan. Olsen called me and let me know. I'm sorry. I know you two were friends."

"Thanks."

"Yeah. Well, um, what I was calling about was that I was wondering when you were going to come in next."

"Come in to the office?"

"Well, yeah. This is an enormously important time, Sam. We've had four detonations, and all have come back as—"

"We had four detonations?" she asked, shocked. She remembered Olsen mentioning that to her, but in her medicated state, it had passed through without the recognition it deserved.

"Oh, well, yeah. I thought you'd heard."

"I'll be right down."

62

Rick stood at his open front door. He didn't move until he heard the door creak in the wind that was blowing through the trees and shrubbery. Walking in, his mouth was dry, and his heart was pounding. He was physically weak and thought, *So this is what being really terrified feels like?*

His gun was upstairs. He walked through the kitchen and into the living room. As he was heading up the stairs, a breeze wafted in, and he saw that the balcony doors were open.

Taking one step at a time, careful not to make them creak, he got to the second floor and glanced down both sides of the hallway before turning into the master bedroom. A framed photo of his wife was on the nightstand. He stared at it a moment and then went to the closet. Up on the top shelf was his 12 gauge. He took down that and a box of ammo. Then he loaded the weapon and cocked it before turning around.

Rick walked back down to the living room. He crossed the carpet, stopping for a moment to listen, and then was about to head out to his kids when he saw something off the balcony—a plume of smoke, several, in fact.

He walked out and slid open the screen. Standing on the balcony, he saw Los Angeles before him, but it didn't resemble any city he'd seen. Fires raged across the city. Some were small patches that produced light, gray smoke, and others were sizeable infernos the length of football fields that discharged a black fog. The streets were clogged with motionless cars, and most shocking of all, he didn't see a single live person. Bodies were everywhere, dotting the landscape like ants over rotting food. Many wore military uniforms.

He heard something in the sky and looked up to see a chopper heading toward downtown. The machine was veering off course, weaving in the air as though it had a drunk driver, far too close to the ground. It squealed as it neared the city and banked downward into a building. A boom and an explosion accompanied it as it slammed into a tower and shattered.

Though Rick was miles away, he flinched. When he opened his eyes again, he saw a smoldering heap of stone and steel where the chopper and fragments of the building had hit the sidewalk.

Rick turned and ran to the RV, grabbing some food and storage water on his way. He ran back to the house twice more, with his kids asking him what was going on, and loaded up as many supplies as he could.

"Dad, what's going on?" his son asked.

He jumped into the driver's seat. "We're getting the hell out of California."

63

Samantha rushed to CDC headquarters. She had asked her nurse to come in early and left her mother and Jessica in her care.

The city was buzzing with activity, and the freeways were packed. Many people had filled their cars to the brim with sleeping bags, clothing, water, and food. A handful of policemen were out, but nowhere near what would be required if all these people decided to start breaking into the closed stores.

Sam listened to NPR, and they were discussing the detonations. Contact had been cut off to Manhattan, Los Angeles, Nashville, and Washington, D.C. Rumors of multiple blasts in Pakistan, China, and all over Europe were circulating. But communications had been disrupted, and getting information was difficult. The internet, it seemed, was down worldwide.

She cut through a field and looped around a business park, avoiding the mess of traffic, and arrived at the CDC in about half an hour.

As she was stepping out of her car, she received the phone call she had been waiting for. "This is Samantha."

"Clyde Olsen, Sam. It's done. Your sister and her family are in Elko, Nevada."

She sighed, all the tension and pain leaving her body. The only remnant was a soft emotional mess. "I don't know how to thank you."

"Figure out how to stop this thing. That's how you can thank me."

By the time she arrived at the CDC, the building was on lockdown, and she had to input a security code at the door. The door hissed and locked behind her. The building was nearly empty. She ran up to Freddy's office but didn't find anyone there. A conference room next door had four people in it; she stepped inside.

"There she is," Freddy said. "Dr. Bower, we were just discussing the potential spread of the pathogen. Please have a seat."

Samantha sat and waited for Freddy to begin speaking again. Up on the whiteboard was a rough drawing of the world. Small X's were written on certain spots.

"Reports are few and far between," Freddy said, taking off his glasses and mopping them with a small white cloth. "But it appears the pathogen can't be contained. We're getting reports from people leaving DC that entire city blocks are filled with the dead or dying. Apparently, it's mutated, and its incubation period has dropped from several days to several hours."

"I don't think that's it," Samantha said.

"Why not?"

"That's too quick a mutation. Although the pathogen mutates faster than anything I've ever seen, it couldn't mutate that quickly. This is a different strain. Something we haven't seen before."

"How do you know?"

"Just a hunch."

"Well, I guess, at this point, we'll take anything." Freddy pointed to two men sitting to Samantha's right. "As far as I know, we don't have any infected in Atlanta yet. See if you two can get some samples from any of the cities, and let's test Sam's theory."

Freddy turned back to the whiteboard and discussed contingency plans, spread ratios, and infectious grid patterns. Sam was barely listening. She knew exactly what everyone in that room was already thinking: it was too late. Too many people in a grid that was too wide had been infected.

The virus would spread from city to city, slowly at first, perhaps over the course of a week. Then the speed of the infections would increase exponentially until it hit a tipping point. The tipping point in an infection pattern was that exact moment when we went from a society *with* infected to a society *of* infected, that point when the death of the species was certain. It takes approximately twelve to fifteen years for a human being to produce an offspring that can then breed—an enormous amount of time, biologically speaking. That was too slow to repopulate the species after the devastation of an extinction-level event.

Most of humanity would be infected within the first three months, and the only ones who wouldn't be were the ones who could get out of the cities in time.

Samantha's head hurt. She put her hand over her eyes and rubbed her temples. "This is pointless."

Freddy stopped and turned to her. "Excuse me?"

"It's out, Freddy. We can't slow it. We can't plan for it. The only thing we can do is hold on and wait until it runs its course." She glanced around the room. "We're not stopping it at this point. We're trying to survive."

64

The building was the tallest one in Miami: the Four Seasons Hotel. Hank Kraski had rented the top suite.

The palatial suite had a bed that appeared to have been made for ten people and a hot tub outside on the massive balcony. Chilled champagne and fresh lobster sat on the table. The suite was exactly the way he had asked.

He sat on the balcony, viewing the city below and the mass of ocean beyond it. He had loved Miami when he was a kid. He could go there and hock stolen baseball cards, packages of gum, or anything he and his friends could get their hands on. Such a shame that it had to be destroyed.

Though it wouldn't be destroyed in the sense that it would be blown apart, but that the people were going to be eliminated. And without the people, there were no maintenance crews to keep the city running smoothly. Nature would need only a few weeks to reclaim what humans had taken.

Hank thought back to his childhood in Florida. He'd been happy with his Polish family that owned a restaurant in downtown Miami. The city had been different then, though, and a small-business owner could thrive without having to take massive loans from predatory banks just to stay afloat. *Such a waste of talent,* he thought. The little guys would get swallowed up or have to work for the big guys, and the consumers suffered. He didn't blame the banks, though. He blamed the government dollars that kept them buoyant when they should have sunk.

But never, in a million years, could he have guessed that he would end up being one of the few people on earth who would survive to rebuild. The new society would be better. It would be more efficient, and the aristocracy would no longer rule the poor. That was why he had such great admiration for the virus. It saw no race, religion, economic status, or fame. The virus was lethal equally and had no regard for anything or anyone. It was… perfect.

His cell phone rang, and he answered. "This is Kraski."

"It's done. They'll be arriving within a few hours."

The line went dead. He placed the phone in his pocket and got the bottle of champagne before returning to the balcony. But, glancing over at the clear waters of the hot tub, he felt the urge to splash around. He stripped down and got in.

He decided that he would watch the end of the world from there.

65

Ngo Chon stood in the glass corridor at the CDC in Atlanta, observing the parking lot as he sipped tea out of a mug that had a saying on the side: Epidemiologists do it disease free.

The CDC. When he was younger, he had dreamed about working there. After medical school, he completed a doctorate and then realized he didn't want to go into the world yet, so he completed another. By the time he got out of school at age thirty-nine, he thought he would be the most educated person at the CDC. He was shocked to find that at least half a dozen people had more degrees than he did, some of them from more prestigious schools.

But he'd outlasted them all. They transferred around, always vying for that position that would bolster their resumes. No matter how much they protested that they had purer motives, it was always about the resume with career academics and scientists. The CV determined the quality of the person.

Chon knew the opposite was probably true. The more crap on the CV, the more likely the person had never done anything new or interesting. Anyone who came up with some interesting theory or project devoted all their time to that one thing. Only when people aimlessly drifted did the CV commence building to the sky, like a nerdy Tower of Babel.

He finished his tea and then headed up to the level four biosafety labs. They were in the most secure facility in the United States, at least that the public knew about—and with good reason. Over a hundred unknown, absolutely lethal hot viruses were frozen in a refrigerated walk-in room on that level. Every so often, a man or woman working for some unknown military unit or spy agency would be flown in to USAMRIID in Maryland. They were typically dead at that point, but he knew of a few live ones. But once they passed, their blood and tissues were analyzed, and if an unknown hot virus was discovered, it went to a freezer on BS4 in Atlanta—even though most CDC employees didn't realize it. USAMRIID also kept the unknown pathogens in BS4 freezers. A room of nightmares was right under their noses, and only a handful of doctors knew about it.

He scrubbed down and checked his suit before pressurizing it and heading into the labs. The room was a cacophony of monkey howls from the twenty or so primates stacked in cages against the wall. Four were lying motionless in pools of blood. They had been injected with black pox—Agent X—less than forty-eight hours ago as a vaccine. The weakened virus husks had flooded their bodies, initiating an immune response that had apparently gone nowhere.

Chon stood frozen, staring at the corpses. *Clever little bastard.*

Samantha thought about staying in her office and finishing up a few of her other cases, but that seemed so pointless as to almost be laughable. A sample of the new strain of Agent X had been flown in and its identity had been confirmed: black pox with a slight mutation that was likely responsible for its hyper-incubation period.

Instead of working in the office, she went to the BS4 labs, stripped and showered, and then put on her suit. She spent a good five minutes searching for tears in the suit before filling it with positive pressure from an air hose connected to the wall. She entered the lab through the decontamination chamber.

Ngo Chon stood there, watching over about twenty specimens of primates, everything from small squirrel monkeys to hundred-and-fifty-pound chimps. Chon didn't notice her and was standing as still as glass, watching the primates.

"No luck?" she asked.

He shook his head in his suit. "I've never seen anything like this. It's not smallpox. With SP, we could vaccinate within a few days and still have positive effects. This thing takes hold in a day. It shuts down the immune system first, uses it to replicate itself. Then it begins attacking healthy cells." He turned to her. "It knows where our defenses are and uses them against us. It's really quite... beautiful in how ferocious it is."

"What progress have we made on a vaccine?"

"Almost none. The virus destroys itself if it's weakened or damaged in any way. Like a self-destruct button, I guess."

She approached one of the cages and stared at a spider monkey that was lying on its side, its breathing heavy as its hands trembled.

It reminded her of the last case of smallpox she had ever seen. Officially, the last known case had occurred in Africa in 1977, but the World Health Organization and the CDC knew that wasn't true. Several cases had been reported in western Africa and parts of South America. But the virus had died out so quickly, the organizations didn't want to raise public alarm.

Sam had gone to Congo during the last outbreak in 2002. A twelve-year-old boy had infected and killed his entire family. She remembered the boy lying much like the monkey was, on his side, a blank expression over his still face as his hands trembled. His skin was coated with pustules that resembled oatmeal.

Smallpox.

"Ngo, how genetically similar is Agent X and its progeny to small pox? Would you say around ninety-nine percent?"

"Yeah, somewhere around there. Why?"

She took a step back. "Because I think I know how to make a vaccine."

66

Six days later, the weakened poxvirus sat in a syringe on her desk as Samantha stared out the window. Requests for aid were coming in from all over the country, but the Centers for Disease Control could provide almost none. The impact was so large that the best they could do was send teams of specialists out with military personnel to assess the damage. But the military wasn't there to heal; they were there to prevent.

In almost every major American city, an order had gone out for isolation. No one was to have contact with anyone else. No school, no work, no church, and no recreational activities. The only way to prevent infection was to avoid exposure to the virus. The hope was that, eventually, the infected would die off.

But humans were social animals, and Sam was even aware of studies in which psychosis ensued after prolonged periods of isolation. She had once spent three weeks by herself in the Sahara after her guide had caught malaria and died. She remembered the madness encroaching like a dark cloud that she could see but couldn't walk away from. It drifted toward her slowly at first, and within two weeks, she was mumbling aloud to herself. The first time she became aware of it, she stopped. But by the second time, she didn't have the strength to fight it anymore. In fact, in some odd way, speaking to herself was comforting.

By the time another guided party happened by and found her, she was having conversations with herself, and learning to stop took several weeks.

Taking up the syringe, she examined the semi-golden fluid within. She tapped it twice to push the bubbles to the top and then placed some pressure on the bottom of the syringe to pop them. Unlike the vast majority of the world's population, she had once been vaccinated for smallpox—before going out into the field. Thinking back, she wondered if that was why she hadn't become infected with Agent X and her old boss, Dr. Ralph Wilson, had. He was a lab worker, not a field worker, and there wouldn't have been a need to vaccinate him.

The chimpanzee she had immunized with smallpox a week ago had grown ill, but he'd survived and was strong. She then injected it with Agent X, and it had survived. The poxvirus wasn't genetically dissimilar enough to prevent a powerful immune response to Agent X. The vaccine had worked once... and it needed a human subject.

She blotted alcohol on her left bicep and then lifted the syringe. It touched the tip of her skin, but before she could push it in, a hand violently jerked it away. Chon stood there, gawking at her. He took the syringe and capped it.

"Come with me."

Samantha followed him up to the BS4 labs, where they suited up. Mongo, the chimp she had injected with smallpox, lay on his side, twitching. Blood pooled around him and was leaking from every orifice in his body. As was also displayed in the human victims, his organs had liquefied and were coming out in thick strands with his feces. Unable to control his bowel movements, he was coated in bloody flesh.

"He didn't display any symptoms," she said.

"Not at first. I took a sample of his blood."

"And?"

"The poxvirus mutated again. I wouldn't have believed it if I didn't see it with my own eyes. But it *sensed* the vaccine, and it mutated."

Samantha knew of only one other virus that could have had such an ability: influenza. The common flu virus was the most adaptable life form on the planet and could almost sense its own destruction. That was why vaccines had to be given every year instead of once in a lifetime: it simply mutated too quickly. But even the flu couldn't mutate within a host after injection of a vaccine.

"Damn," she muttered. She began pacing. "This is the key, Ngo. There has to be some way to slow the mutation."

"How?"

She thought of graduate school. She remembered an experiment in which they slowed ants with liquid nitrogen. When they thawed, they would pick up exactly where they had left off. If they were heading for a piece of food, they would continue there. If they were retreating, that's what they would continue doing.

"What if we could slow the mutation with liquid nitrogen? After immunization with poxvirus, we could slow Agent X before injection. Maybe that would give the body enough time to come up with antibodies before the next mutation?"

Ngo thought it over. "I love it. I'll get the LN. We have some in Lab Two."

Samantha bent down in front of Mongo. She placed her thickly gloved hand over his head, and he didn't have the strength to respond. Instead, he whimpered and closed his eyes.

67

Tommy Metheny stood in line outside for his portion of the rations. The San Antonio heat pounded down on his head so fiercely that he kept having to mop his face with the back of his arm. The grocery stores had been wiped clean. He'd gone that morning, and nothing was left, not even batteries. The employees had abandoned the store, and the big chains had given up, too. The only ones still left were the mom-and-pop stores, and the owners guarded their inventory with shotguns and pistols.

One of his neighbors had been robbed overnight. He called the police, but no one came. The police, he'd heard, couldn't go out on calls anymore. Tommy didn't understand why some fucking terrorist attack in Manhattan and LA had to affect him. Those places were in different worlds. Let them worry about it. Wasn't that what he paid his taxes for? Instead, he was out there in hundred-degree heat just to get a few military rations so he could feed his wife and kids.

The soldiers had taken over an old rec center, and he stood by the entrance. Four hours, he'd waited, and as he approached, a woman in a uniform stepped out of the building. She had a cold, determined look on her face. The kind that was meant to deliver bad news and give the impression that she didn't give a shit that she was the one delivering it.

"We're sorry," she bellowed, "but that's all the rations we will be handing out today."

She continued to speak, but no one heard her. The crowd was in an uproar. Tommy was yelling, too.

"This what I pay my fucking taxes for, huh? This what I paid 'em for twenty years for?"

The shouting grew more intense and someone Tommy couldn't see tried to push the woman out of the way of the entrance and go inside. The woman was young, probably inexperienced, and not well trained. She should have locked the doors and gone for help. But she went for the pistol holstered at her side. One of the men in line swung at her, a wide haymaker that connected to her jaw. The blow was so hard, Tommy heard the pop of her jaw as she fell back and hit her head on the cement.

The crowd rushed in through the doors, ripping the remaining rations from the arms of the young soldiers. Only three of them had been stationed there. Tommy was unclear which one did it first, but at some point, they removed their semi-automatic rifles, and opened fire on the crowd.

Tommy ran out of the rec center, holding four ration containers. The pop of gunfire followed him, and off in the distance, a military truck was speeding toward them. He had no plans on sticking around for that.

As he turned to go to his car, a rumbling tore through the air. The sound was so deep and forceful that he felt the vibration in his bones, as if he'd been holding a powerful jackhammer that hit something unbreakable.

The crowds were quieted and stood still. Even the military vehicle had stopped. Tommy saw that everyone's faces were turned to the sky. An eerie feeling gave him shivers. People had been ready to tear each other's throats out one second, and the next, they stopped and gazed up. He almost didn't want to know what would make them do that.

A shadow moved over him, and he turned, looked up to the blue sky... and screamed.

Scourge, Book III in the Plague Trilogy, coming Spring 2014

AUTHOR'S REQUEST

If you enjoyed this book, please leave a review on Amazon. Good reviews not only encourage authors to write more, they improve our writing. Shakespeare rewrote sections of his plays based on audience reaction and modern authors should take a note from the Bard.

So please leave a review and know that this author appreciates each and every one of you!

BY VICTOR METHOS

Plague Trilogy

Plague (A Medical Thriller)

Pestilence

Scourge (Coming February 2014)

Thrillers

Diary of an Assassin

Black Sky (A Mystery-Thriller)

Murder Corporation (A Crime Thriller)

Superhero Thrillers

Superhero (An Action Thriller)

Black Onyx

Black Onyx Reloaded

Jon Stanton Thrillers

The White Angel Murder

Walk in Darkness

Sin City Homicide

Arsonist

The Porn Star Murders

Sociopath

Creature-Feature Novels

The Extinct

Sea Creature

Paranormal Thrillers

Dracula (A Modern Telling)

Savage: A Novel

Science Fiction & Fantasy

Clone Hunter

Star Dreamer: The Early Science Fiction of Victor Methos

Empire of War

Humor

Earl Lindquist: Accountant and Zombie Killer

Philosophical Fiction

Existentialism and Death on a Paris Afternoon

To contact the author, learn about his latest adventures, get tips on starting your own adventures, or learn about upcoming releases, please visit the author's blog at http://methosreview.blogspot.com/